W9-BZW-142

Stronger than you know

Stronger than you know

JOLENE PERRY

Albert Whitman & Company
Chicago, Illinois

Library of Congress Cataloging-in-Publication Data

Perry, Jolene B. (Jolene Betty).
Stronger than you know by / Jolene Perry.
pages cm
Summary: After fifteen years of horrific abuse and neglect by her mother and her
mother's boyfriends, Joy struggles to understand and accept a normal life with relatives,
at school, and with a boyfriend.
[1. Emotional problems—Fiction. 2. Child abuse—Fiction. 3. Sexual abuse—Fiction.
4. Family life—Fiction. 5. High schools—Fiction. 6. Schools—Fiction.
7. Psychotherapy—Fiction.] I. Title.
PZ7.P4349Str 2014
[Fic]—dc23

Text copyright © 2014 by Jolene Perry
Published in 2014 by Albert Whitman & Company
ISBN 978-0-8075-3155-6 (hardcover)

Printed in China.
10 9 8 7 6 5 4 3 2 1 NP 18 17 16 15 14

Cover design by Jenna Stempel
Cover image © Jessica Neuwerth Photography/Getty Images

For more information about Albert Whitman & Company,
visit our web site at www.albertwhitman.com.

TO EMMA ROSE and JACK MICHAEL

MAY YOU ALWAYS KNOW HOW MUCH YOU ARE LOVED

CHILD SERVICES SUMMARY REPORT

NAME: Joy Neilsons
AGE: 15
CASE WORKER: Louisa Gray

FINDINGS: (a brief compilation from both physician and psychiatrist)
- Severe signs of abuse and neglect.
- Victim was not often allowed outside of 750 sq. ft. mobile home.
- She did not attend school but had received schooling through the home school system.
- Neighbors believed her to be an occasional guest of the residence but not a permanent fixture. Victim explained that occasionally months would go by when she was not allowed outside.
- Approximately 10–15 lbs. underweight. Dehydrated. Malnourished.

CURRENT STATUS:
- Inpatient care.
- Solitary room as victim panics around men and is silent and shaking in groups—both have led to panic attacks in the few days since admittance.
- Waiting for aunt to retrieve victim. Home study and background check of aunt, uncle, and cousins completed.
- Mother (defendant) and boyfriend (defendant) are currently in California state custody.

LARGEST CONCERNS:
- Depression—possibly suicidal
- Anxiety
- Integration into functioning society will be overwhelming. Until this point she has coped mostly by hiding and causing as little disruption as possible. Becoming part of a family or student group will be challenging at best.

ONE

THREE MONTHS IN AND NO LESS BROKEN THAN BEFORE

I read somewhere that happiness is fleeting, but joy sticks with you, holds on to you, and fills you up. The fact that my name is Joy is sort of a lesson in irony.

I sit here because I'm still broken. I'll probably always sit in offices like this, because I'll probably always be broken.

Dr. Mayar—no, wait, *Lydia*—is waiting for my response.

"Joy?"

"What?" I wait for her to repeat the question, hoping to buy myself more time. We meet for forty-five minutes twice a week. It's a game to see how many minutes I can waste. The more time we say nothing, the less time we have to talk about things I don't want to talk about.

Her body doesn't move, her face doesn't change, but I can feel the disapproval sliding toward me in waves. "I know you heard me. One thing, Joy. One. You can do this."

You can do this, she says. It's so ridiculous. It's not like I'm lifting weights or anything. Like she's my coach, yelling from the sidelines, "One more set, one more! Push yourself! I know you can do it!"

What muscle am I exercising here? My brain? My heart? A combination of the two? Because it feels like a lot more of me is broken than just that. I mean, where do I even start? The thoughts swim around inside me so fast that I can't catch them or formulate them into something I can grasp, understand, or deal with.

"Joy, I know you're watching the clock, because you're always watching the clock when we're close to time. But, you're not leaving until you can tell me one thing you like about yourself." Her dark, narrow face is fixed on me.

This is probably the cheesiest thing ever. She asks me to come up with something often. "You have another appointment," I say. She can't wait forever.

She leaves herself ten minutes between appointments to make notes and prepare for the next. I know this. It means her time with me is limited. And that gives me confidence about my ability to drag this out to the point where I won't have to answer.

"Not today." She recrosses her legs and leans back in her chair. Sometimes I sit in here and just stare at her dark African skin. It's beautiful, like she glows from within. Were things harder for her because of her skin? I'm not sure. In fifteen years my pale skin hasn't helped me any.

I pull my arms more tightly around my legs. I look too much like my mom for me to pick something about myself that I like. Same straight brown hair. Same tiny little button nose that I hate. I'm too skinny, but so is Mom. Or she was the last time I saw her.

My head rests to the side to look at myself in Lydia's tiny mirror. I even have Mom's brown eyes.

"Okay, Joy, I'm not talking *physical* traits here. You know this. Give me something else. Anything." The annoyance she's trying to hide in her voice makes me hold in a grin.

"I'm smart. I don't need my teachers to tell me how to do things."

She chuckles. "I'm impressed. That was a good one." She runs a hand through her short, spiky black hair as she leans back in her chair. I love making her smile; her teeth are perfectly straight and white.

I thought it was a good one too. But then I realize, in a way, that it's a dig at my teachers.

I blink in the chair and feel suddenly that I'm back at my first day of school. I'd never seen so many people in one place. Mom's trailer would get packed once in a while, but nothing like the jumping and hollering and the sea of navy, white, and khaki that awaited me in the halls.

I looked at all the faces, the smiling faces, the groups, the kids who sat reading, the kids who sat playing on their phones, and I had no idea how or where I fit into any of it. I still don't.

"How are we doing with talking?" Lydia asks, bringing me back to the present.

"I'm talking now." I let my eyes rest on hers. I've been to a lot of shrinks since Mom was taken to jail. A lot. Shrinks that specialize in child abuse, that specialize in neglect. I've been to people who work only in physical abuse cases and people who counsel teens with depression and anxiety issues. I fall under every category. Lucky me. I see Lydia because she's close to my aunt and uncle's house. She grew up in foster homes after her mom was sent to jail, so she gets at least a small part of me.

"Please don't make me run around in circles again to get what we both know I'm after. You've been with your aunt and uncle for three months, right?"

"Yeah."

"And have you and your aunt talked much about what brought you to them?"

"No more than we did when I sat here last week. She has my file. I don't get to choose what she does or doesn't know about me." I hate that I don't get to choose what she knows. Sometimes I wonder if she read it all right away, or if it she thought, *okay, ten minutes on the horrible life of Joy tonight, and I'll do ten more minutes tomorrow. My, it'll take me a long time to get done with this large file.*

"But your mom is her sister. And I think she'd like to hear things from *you*."

I disagree with Lydia on this count. Aunt Nicole drove to California to pick me up when child services called her. She barely spoke to me for fifteen hours on the drive back to her house. Maybe she was in shock, but she couldn't have been more in shock than me.

"Why don't we…" Lydia's eyes go back to her clock, and I have to wonder if she was lying earlier when she said her following appointment canceled. "This is what I want you to do this week—ready?"

I just stare. This is the part of our visit that I dread. The *homework* part. Only she doesn't let me call it that.

"Talk to your uncle, share something with him."

I open my mouth to protest, but she holds her hand up between us.

"It can be something as simple as telling him about someone at school, okay? Anything."

"It's not like I'm the *silent* kid." But my hands shake at the thought of talking to Uncle Rob.

"You're *almost* the silent kid."

"Fine." I'm saying this just to appease her. I grab a strand of plain brown hair to give my hands something to do aside from shake and pull it in front of me to look for split ends like my cousin, Tara, is always doing. It gives me some time when I don't have to see the expectant face of Lydia. I know I'll just let her down. It's rare I'm able to do what she asks of me during the week.

I try to tell myself I'm doing better than my first few weeks with my aunt and uncle. I never knew what to say but I tried so hard. I was filled with yeahs and uh-huhs. It was so exhausting to try to figure out when I was supposed to talk and when I wasn't that I gave up— at least for a while. Mom was happy when I stayed silent and hid in my room.

"And I want you to talk to someone at school. Give one of your friends some kind of detail about you. And no, neither of your cousins count, and your teachers don't either." She smirks. Her weird smile is how she tries to lighten the mood.

My chest sinks. It's overwhelming, which is stupid. It's just that I don't really have *friends* friends. I mean, when I sit in the cafeteria, I sit with Tara's friends, but they're not really my friends. Trent, her twin, is always inviting his sports team over, and their loud voices and the way they push each other around...I don't like guys in groups.

"Joy? Why does this make you nervous?"

I push out a frustrated burst of air. "I don't know what to say to people. I don't know how to answer their questions or..." But I just trail off because I'm not sure how to continue. Even with Lydia I don't feel like I can say—*when Mom had a group of people over, I got too much attention from the guys there. I don't like men.* Why aren't there more all-girl private schools near Seattle?

"Why don't you play around with some things to tell people about why you're in your aunt and uncle's house? Nothing that's a lie, but maybe something that would satisfy curiosity. We've talked about this before, but I don't think you came up with anything more than you moved from California."

"I'll think about it." Maybe.

Now I get to leave. I think we had eight minutes of silence today. Eight minutes when I didn't have to speak and I didn't have to listen to her say things that make me want to run out of her office.

"How are you feeling with your meds?"

I shrug.

Since I was pulled from my house, they've all been sure I'm going to off myself. The docs stuck me on the depression meds almost as soon as I checked in. Maybe they just weren't sure what else to do.

"Let me know if you think something needs to change."

I turn to face her before grabbing the door handle. "You're the doctor."

"And I'm relying on you to tell me how you feel." We have this interchange every time we see each other.

"Fine. I'm fine."

"Joy." Her voice has that tone of seriousness that makes me pause. "I know you feel like you're not moving forward, so I'd like you to do one *easy* thing for me. Write me an email or write in your journal about what it was like when your Aunt Nicole first picked you up. Keep it simple. Talk about any part of that experience you want to, but you'll see how far you've come in a very short time."

I step out of Lydia's office overwhelmed with what she wants me to do this week. The letter or journal thing is fine, but the other two tasks seem impossible, which makes me feel stupid. She's basically asked me to say one thing to my uncle and one thing to someone I know at school.

I'm Joy, the girl who's so broken that the thought of speaking two sentences is making it hard to breathe.

TWO

MY ASSIGNMENT FROM LYDIA

I sketch in the margins of the paper instead of working on my writing assignment, but something about drawing again makes me think of my trailer home. I scratch it all out, flip to a clean sheet of paper, and start to write.

There was no way to fill fifteen hours in the car with my Aunt Nicole, who I'd never met. I didn't attempt to fill the silence because I had no idea how or even if I should.

I also didn't know how to process the landscape. The cities, the small towns, the gas stations, the ocean. It felt too enormous to possibly be real. Like the National Geographic Channel come to life around me.

Over the week before Aunt Nicole arrived, I'd been taken from the trailer where I'd spent nearly every minute of my life, locked in a small room, and asked to relive almost every experience I'd had while with my mom.

Aunt Nicole asked me about a million times if I was okay. If I wanted to stop for the bathroom. If I wanted food. She was always trying to feed me, but she kept getting these enormous bags from McDonald's, and I couldn't risk spilling crumbs in her car.

I still feel this way. So far, this assignment isn't helping any.

I throw that last line in for good measure.

I ate very little. At home Mom usually had frozen pizzas for me, or sometimes I'd open a can of soup or chili.

I'm starting to realize how crazy it was that I ate at night after Mom was asleep. Or I'd get up after she went to work and eat standing over the sink so I wouldn't have to clean crumbs off the table.

Hours went by and we were still driving. How big was the world? How many places could there be? How far apart was everything? It was crazy to think about how enormous the world was as we kept driving.

Now that I have a grasp of what a short distance we actually traveled, that too makes me feel stupid.

I knew Aunt Nicole's house was just a house, but it was so big and too pretty—I couldn't imagine myself belonging in a place like that.

I pulled my knees to my chest and wrapped my arms around my legs, closing my eyes tight for a moment. The house and the kindness and...everything...were too much. Aunt Nicole talked to me like I was a three-year-old, which I probably deserved, asking me to please leave the car, and told me about how great everything would be with my uncle and cousins and a new city to explore.

I nearly left the car when she promised privacy inside. Said I had a bathroom attached to my room even.

There were so many nights at home when I had to pee desperately, but Mom had people over and I didn't want to be noticed. Walking across the hall was a sure way to get attention.

I actually asked Aunt Nicole if I could sleep in the car. That's how desperate I was to not move. I don't write about begging to sleep in the car to Lydia because it makes me feel ridiculous—especially now that I've been there for three months, and the house is no longer scary. But I guess that's the point of the assignment. To show me how far I've come. I'm reluctant to admit my progress, even to myself.

Aunt Nicole sat just outside my car door when she remembered that she'd forgotten to give me my Xanax before we arrived. (I hate those by the way. They make me sleepy and rubbery.)

We made a deal though, before leaving California. If Aunt Nicole handed me a pill, I had to take it, and I was given a number to call if I felt like it was happening too much or if I was uncomfortable with anything going on in the house. It's sort of stupid, really. I was burned and hit and, AND...

I can't say the word. Not even in a journal. It feels too horrible.

...in my last house, and I never called anyone. It seems kind of ignorant on the part of the child services people to tell me to call if something doesn't feel right. I had no idea what to expect. Or what was normal. I'd only just learned that my normal wasn't normal at all.

I knew even then that my fear of that house might be ridiculous, but I didn't know how to shake it. All I had was unknown—unknown cousins, unknown uncle, and an aunt I'd just met.

The moment we reached the porch, the front door opened to

expose a man several inches taller than Mom's last boyfriend, Richard, and I froze.

I make sure I write the Uncle Rob stuff because maybe Lydia won't force me to talk to him after reading this.

When I saw my Uncle Rob all I could think was please no. I know what he'll want, and I'm not big enough to stop him. Aunt Nicole can't have more power than my mom to stop a man that large.

Aunt Nicole threw herself into his arms and they murmured so quietly I felt like I shouldn't listen. A part of me registered that I thought my aunt was nice and that she liked him, so maybe he wasn't bad. But he was a man I didn't know in a house I didn't know, and maybe certain things were going to be expected of me. A lot had been expected of me in the past. I had no reason to believe that Uncle Rob was any different.

Uncle Rob said hello or something equally simple, but the lowness of his voice felt like a warning. Run. Hide. Only I couldn't just run away. I had no idea where I was.

It was awful. New house. New man. New situation that I was sure would turn out like my old one. I don't even have to exaggerate to show what a mess I was. This assignment isn't making me feel better. It's making me feel worse because I still don't want to share space with my uncle.

Aunt Nicole was nice enough to see how awful I felt and she sent Uncle Rob inside. (This is all making me feel crazier by the way.) Aunt Nicole brought me through a massive foyer in a house so big that my trailer could have fit in the kitchen. She led me up stairs three times wider than the hallway at home and into a room with its own bathroom.

My room.

That first night will always be etched in my memory. I dropped my backpack and went through the doorway and into my own bathroom. Tears spilled down my face at the glimpse of a life I knew I didn't belong in.

THREE
KEEPING TRACK

Every time I do something that puts me out of my comfort zone, I write it down. This way when I see Lydia, I can hand her my notebook and she can see how well I'm doing. Also, if I don't do my writing assignment, I at least have something to show her. The problem is that my lists always look the same. Almost every week. The same, simple things still put me on edge.

> ○ *Went to school.*
> ○ *Ate in the cafeteria.*
> ○ *Answered a teacher's question.*
> ○ *Ate a few bites of dinner with the family in the dining room.*

I hardly eat anything in the cafeteria, but I don't write that.

Today, I'm wearing a white short-sleeved button-up shirt with my tan uniform pants. I think some of the cigarette burn marks might even show. They're just white spots now, but it should still count. I add it to the list.

○ *Wore short-sleeved shirt to school.*

I feel like if I do this, maybe Lydia won't be too upset with me for not talking to someone at school or to my uncle. I don't plan on doing either.

"Morning." Aunt Nicole smiles from the kitchen as I step downstairs. Her brown hair flies around her as she spins in the massive kitchen.

I give her a small wave.

"You look pretty today." She bounces from the fridge to the toaster to the cupboards as she gets breakfast ready.

My aunt and her family are such a normal all-American family that it's not normal at all. Even the families on TV aren't like them. I'm guessing they have their minor problems like everyone, but I've never seen any arguments. It's rare that we don't have dinner as a family. Or that *they* don't have dinner as a family. I sneak down when everyone's in bed to eat.

Aunt Nicole stays home, supports her husband, and attends every school function. The house is always in some state of clean. Everything about her and their three-story home in this picture-perfect neighborhood is so different from the trailer I grew up in. Even after three months, I'm not used to it.

"I have an appointment downtown. Rob's going to drive you guys today," Aunt Nicole says. "Because we need to get the oil changed in Trent and Tara's car, and…"

I don't hear what else she says. Uncle Rob. That won't work. My heart's already frantic at the thought of being with him in a small space. I can't do it. No way. I don't care if saying something to him is one of my goals this week. If I find it within myself to be able to speak to him, it isn't going to be within the confines of a car.

I turn to the door. "I planned on walking, but thanks." My backpack is already over my shoulder, and my shoes are already on. My heart's beating hard, and my ribs are too tight to take a deep breath.

Aunt Nicole stands in silence, watching me from the kitchen. I can hear Uncle Rob's deep, low, voice with his two kids in the dining room. That's close enough. All I want is to get to school. Alone.

"Joy?" Aunt Nicole walks up behind me.

I open the door before I decide that I really need to turn around and face her. "It's a nice day. I'll walk." My heart's thrumming, faster, more frantic. Space, I just need a little space. And more air. Why does air get harder to breathe when all I want is a deep breath?

"But, breakfast." Aunt Nicole looks almost just like my mom—same build, same brown eyes and hair—but her kindness makes her look so much softer.

How do I tell her that the simple idea of riding in a car with her husband has ruined my appetite? My day's barely begun, and already I have tears threatening the edges of my eyes.

"Take this." She holds out a piece of toast. "And I can drive you right now. I don't mind."

"I'd rather walk." I reach for the toast, even though I'm not sure I'll eat it. "Thanks for breakfast."

The day is warm. It's fall in Seattle, which I'm learning comes with a lot of rain. But not today. Today is beautiful.

Even though I'm halfway down the driveway, I can hear Aunt Nicole sigh behind me. Really it just adds to my guilt. I've taken over their extra bedroom and just added worry to their perfectly normal life. I take two bites of toast and drop the rest in a bush. A squirrel will probably eat it within the hour. My heart's back to normal and my lungs are working the way they should. The walk was a good idea.

"You really shouldn't waste food like that," says a guy behind me.

My heart immediately takes off. I don't turn—just keep walking. Maybe if I don't say anything else, he'll go away.

"Joy, right?"

My body jumps again. What do I do? My fingertips feel numb and suddenly I suck in another breath. Was I holding my breath?

"Hey, I'm Justin. We're in government together." His voice is relaxed and friendly. This should be like talking to Trent, right? I've said a few words to my cousin before.

"Right."

I said something. It came out in a rush of breath, but I talked. I wonder if this gets me off the hook with Lydia.

"I didn't know you walked." He keeps pace with me. "To school, I mean. I walk every day. I just got my license, but my dad won't relinquish his car to me." He chuckles. It's like he doesn't care that I'm not really talking back. Or looking at him.

I wrap my arms tightly around my front, as if it will somehow protect me from someone I probably don't need protection from. *Probably.* Now I can't take a deep breath. I need a bench or something before I pass out.

There's a city bus stop just ahead. My chest begs for more air that I'm not sure I can give it. *I can make it. I can make it. Just a few more steps to the bench.* I suck in a breath, but it doesn't come in as far as I need and sounds all funny, wheezy. This is not good. Why am I being followed today? I don't want an audience. Not for this.

"Are you okay?" Justin leans forward.

Brown hair falls over his dark eyes.

My legs almost knock on the wood as I sit and lean forward, resting my elbows on my knees.

"Joy, you're kind of scaring me here." He sits, but keeps his distance. He still feels too close. At least he didn't try to touch me or anything. "Maybe you're sick or something. Can I walk you home?" His voice is nice. Not deep, but definitely guy. He sounds so worried. That's the number one emotion I seem to pull from people.

"I'm..." I suck in a breath. "I sometimes have a hard time breathing."

"Like asthma or something?"

Wow. That's perfect. I nod. Asthma is a lot less insane than panic attacks.

"Don't you have an inhaler?" He's leaning forward trying to see my face again. "I'm starting to freak out a little."

I shake my head. My long hair hangs between us. I can just see his shape through the brown.

"Why don't I walk with you back home, okay?"

My breathing does sound terrible. If I saw someone hunched over her lap on a bench, I'd freak out too.

I stand slowly and start to walk. At this point, home sounds like my best option. Why do I keep insisting I'm ready for school?

"Can I get your bag for you?" A hand touches my shoulder.

My heart jumps with my body. "I'm okay." But my eyes catch his dark ones again. There's nothing but worry there. So now I know I'm overreacting to everything, but I don't know how to *stop* overreacting. Instead I keep walking. I'm next to guys at school all day and I can deal with it. They just never *talk* to me.

"I was just going to offer to take your bag, that's all. To help you breathe." His hand is still outstretched.

"Okay, just don't…touch me." That would make things worse.

He shrugs like it's a totally normal request. "Okay."

I slide the backpack off my shoulder and he catches it as we walk. "Thanks." That was just me, saying something totally voluntary to a guy. I sort of want to *call* Lydia. Does it count if I'm having a small version of a panic attack while doing talking to someone? Maybe that'll get her off my back in the stretching-boundaries department. This whole humiliating experience could work to my advantage.

Aunt Nicole's small white car pulls over. I'm saved. Completely and totally *saved*. The window rolls down. "You okay, Joy?"

"Her asthma was acting up," Justin offers.

"Oh," she says. We both know I don't have asthma.

"Here's your bag. Maybe I'll see you later." He stands there for another moment before walking away. He's not a big guy, only a couple inches taller than me. It makes him less...scary.

"Thank you!" Aunt Nicole calls out.

"Justin," I whisper.

"Justin!"

I let myself look up to see him wave before he walks around the corner, a piece of his dark hair falling over one eye. He's cute. Really cute. Even though I hope he never talks to me again, I can appreciate that about him.

"Climb in," she says through the window.

I open the door and sit in the familiar smell of her car. Just Aunt Nicole and me—this I can do. My body begins to relax. First my chest and shoulders, then the cage around my lungs.

Aunt Nicole digs in her purse. "I have your Xanax in here, but if you want to go to school, it might not be the best idea to take one now..." She stops digging and her eyes meet mine. "I'm going to let you decide this time. Do you want one of your pills to help you calm down?"

My breathing already feels better so I shake my head.

"Okay." She drops her purse on the floor. "I can take you home, but Rob's there today, and I know he makes you uncomfortable."

I put my hands on my cheeks as they heat up. I hate that she knows this. We drive in silence for a few minutes that feel more like an hour.

"Joy, you know Rob would never hurt you, right?"

I nod and focus on the smoothness of the gray dashboard. "That's why I feel so stupid about being…afraid."

"Oh, honey…don't. Don't feel like that." Her voice is always so friendly. No matter what crazy thing I've done, or how her schedule is arranged or rearranged for me, she maintains her friendly voice. I sometimes wonder if it's a struggle or if she's naturally this nice. How did she and my mom turn out so different?

And how can I not feel stupid when logic tells me one thing, but every other part of my body tells me something different?

I'm totally interrupting her morning over nothing. "I'm sorry about this. I just…"

"It's kind of a big deal that you let that boy walk with you." Her voice is so encouraging—especially for something as simple as walking with someone.

"Except he's the one that brought on the panic attack." That means our exchange probably doesn't even count as me moving forward. He does totally count as talking to someone at school, though.

"Well, you said a few things, right?"

"Yeah…A few…" I'm just not sure where exactly a panic attack because of a few words exchanged falls on the crazy scale of one to ten. A five? An eight? Maybe it depends on how insane a full ten really is.

"Why don't we find somewhere to get breakfast? My appointment shouldn't take long, and then you can decide if you're ready to go to school." Her voice is so calm, relaxed. As if I freak out on the way to school every day, and I'm just one more thing on her list of things to do. No big deal.

Make breakfast.

Check.

Pick up Joy hyperventilating on the sidewalk with a stranger.

Check.

Offer to get Joy breakfast on the way to school to ease anxiety.

Check.

"No breakfast, and I'm so sorry." The words come out in a mumble. "It's like I've completely disrupted...everything here."

Aunt Nicole reaches out to touch me, but stops. And it sucks because I actually wouldn't mind. Though I really don't need to be thinking about wanting things that are out of my reach.

"Joy, don't ever think that. I already can't imagine you not in our house. It's like we didn't even know you were missing until you got here."

I shake my head. She's way too nice. Aunt Nicole is just really good at knowing what to say.

"It's up to you whether you believe me or not, but it's how I feel. I love you. I missed way too much of your life. It feels good to have you around." No matter how nice and soft and *understanding* she seems, I'm still afraid to trust her words. No one would think taking me in is no big deal.

I pull my legs onto the seat, completely overwhelmed. She's said things like this before, but it feels like it means even more on a morning when I've completely disrupted her routine.

"So, do you want to hang out with me today? Or are you ready to face school?" Aunt Nicole asks.

"I can go." As much as I'd love to spend the day with her, I know she's busy. She's just being nice again.

We drive in silence for a few minutes.

"Did we push you too hard to be in school this fall?"

"No," I answer immediately.

"It just seems like..."

"I feel insane enough already. Keeping me home from school would just make it worse." I can't believe I just admitted that.

"You're not..." But she doesn't finish. Right. She knows it as well as I do. "Here we are." She stops in front of the main doors.

I climb out of the car, but hold the door open. My chest is a little heavy from her near admission of my mental state.

"Do you need a note?" she asks.

"I'm a pink-slip kid, remember?" My pink slip is my reward for being a mental case.

"Right."

Pink-slip kids have a free pass to get out of class and go to the counselor. If I'm late or if I need to leave early, I can do that too. The catch is that the office immediately calls my aunt and uncle every time I use it. Then there are questions from my aunt and uncle about why I left last period early or if I'm okay or do I need to schedule an appointment with Lydia. Even when the questions are unspoken, they rattle through my head. Aunt Nicole's eyes seem to hold an endless list of things she might like to know.

FOUR
STILL DON'T WORK RIGHT

"You made it."

I lift my eyes from the floor to see Justin at his desk.

He sits *next* to me in U.S. Government? How did I not notice?

"Yeah." My gaze falls back to the floor. Much safer.

"Got your inhaler?"

"What?" Oh. Right. So I can either say something and let him in on more than I've even told my cousins or go for the lie. "Yep. My inhaler."

I'm *totally* off the hook for talking to a student.

His eyes rest on me for too long. I may be looking down, but I'm good at still seeing what's going on. I run my hand through my hair and rest it behind my ear so I can see Justin more clearly without looking at him directly.

I open my book to where my assignment is tucked away from yesterday.

Justin shifts the books on his desk. He doesn't even have an inkling of my past—my crazy mom in jail, the men she brought home. None of it. All he knows is that I live with my cousins and go to this school. Maybe I could tell him one real thing. Maybe.

His fingers tap his forehead in concentration as he frantically finishes his assignment before our teacher asks for them. I open my mouth to speak, but nothing comes out and nothing comes to mind. Well, maybe I could tell him one real thing later.

I feel bad for lying to him about having asthma, so I hand him my assignment so he can get the last answers down. Our teacher still has his nose in attendance.

"Thanks. I'm almost toast in this class." His eyes hit mine again, and there's a warm, fuzzy sort of feeling in my chest and buzzing around my insides. How can something as simple as a look make me feel so much?

I tuck my hair behind my ear again as I watch him copy the answers. My stomach and chest and everything else feel all funny so I stare at my desk.

Then I let my eyes float around the room because maybe always staring at my desk is strange.

There are so many people. A sea of school uniforms. Why does the number of people in a room lock my ribs together and make them shrink? Yeah, not ready for that. My focus goes back to my desk. It's easier to deal with. The fake wood grain seems like such a waste of…something.

"So I know our school can be a little crazy. How are things?" Tara spins around to face me from the passenger's seat. She and Trent share this car. I have no idea why we needed a ride this morning but have a car this afternoon. I'm sort of on the periphery, hovering around the family—I only sort of know what's going on.

"Okay." I know my answer is the same answer I always give her, but she doesn't seem to mind.

"You have Mr. Witten for math, right?" she asks.

I nod.

"Yeah, I had him last year. He always put me to sleep." She smirks.

I'd be sunk if I didn't know how to teach myself.

"Trent has basketball season coming up. You totally need to come to some of the games. I mean, I know you missed out on all that because your mom used to home-school you. He's really good." Tara's voice has a perpetual edge of suspense to it. Instead of making me nervous, I find her interesting to listen to.

Trent chuckles in the driver's seat. "I'm in the starting line-up this year."

He's the teen version of his dad. Light brown hair, blue-gray eyes. But he's still gangly while his dad is broader. Funny that I can ride in a car with Trent, but not his dad. Or maybe the idea that Trent is less scary is just ridiculous. It should probably go on my list of crazy.

"As you should be. Our senior year." Tara gives her brother a friendly slug on the shoulder. Their family is like *The Brady Bunch*.

Mom used to watch TV all the time—loved the really old shows from the fifties, sixties, seventies. She always told me how fake they were. I believed her until I moved in with the Mooresons.

Now Tara and Trent are chatting about things I don't understand and people I don't know. I'm sure Aunt Nicole and Uncle Rob have talked to them about me, my past, or whatever, but I doubt my cousins know much. It makes me wonder what they tell their friends at school. Did Lydia give them a line? Or did she pull them aside, like she did with me, so they could come up with their own lie.

Mom home-schooled me. That's what Tara says. The thought is actually a little funny. I home-schooled myself. I talked to Aunt Nicole when I was about eight and had never gone to school. Aunt Nicole said school was a big deal and that I should talk to my mom about it.

Mom was dating a decent guy at the time. One who left me alone. He took Mom to the school district to sign me up for home school. Once I was signed up for one year, registering for the next year was a lot easier. I filled out the forms every fall and kept myself in school. Without the movie *Matilda*, I wonder if I would have ever attempted to learn or study anything. The number of times I tried to make things happen using my mind so I could be more like her...

Sadness sweeps over me. It never worked—moving things with my mind. No matter how hard I concentrated. I was never able to keep Mom from drinking. I wasn't able to keep the people out of our house that she'd invite over. I wasn't able to keep myself from getting hurt. Over and over.

I lay my head back against the headrest and I stare at the ceiling of the car, letting my tears pool up on the edges of my eyes. Hopefully they'll soak back in before we stop. Leaning forward right now would make them spill over. I don't want to cry in front of my cousins. I don't want to cry in front of anyone. Actually, while I'm wishing, I don't want to cry at all.

"Dinner!" Aunt Nicole calls.

I'm already in the dining room. Like maybe if I'm still enough or quiet enough, no one will notice me. I'm hungry today and dying for dinner, which is why I'm here. Uncle Rob cracks open a beer. My spine freezes. Trent grabs a sip when his dad sets it down and gets a dirty look for it.

The smell hits my nose. That's it. My stomach clenches up, and it takes everything I have to not fall into a panic attack right at the table. Beer and cigarette smoke. Nothing takes me back to that horrible place like the smell.

The Mooresons' house disappears. The dining room turns into dingy white walls, thick cigarette smoke, and the stale beer breath of the last man who lived with us. He was by far the worst of them.

"Joy?" Aunt Nicole asks. "Are you okay?"

But their house and my old house all swim together in a mess I can't sort out.

I stand up and run out of the dining room before the picture of *him* takes over my mind, and then, because I'm crazy, takes over my body. Guilt runs through me, on top of feeling stupid. I know Aunt Nicole worked on dinner for a long time. I run up the stairs to the room, closing the door behind me.

I shove the man's face from my memory. I don't want him there. One day we'll have the technology to erase memories, and he's where I'll start.

After a few minutes in the quiet, my heart slows. There's nothing in here from my old life. Louisa, the social worker from Bakersfield, California, thought I might want something from the trailer Mom and I had called home, but I didn't. I even threw away the clothes I wore the day I left.

The new room I stay in is clean. The walls are a soft green. The trim and shelves are white. The bed is white. The comforter is white. Aunt Nicole offered to change it for me, but I declined. It feels sterile, safe. I sit on the beige carpet, my legs crossed in front of me.

Footsteps on the stairs about ten minutes later, and I'm sure it's Aunt Nicole coming to check on me.

"Joy? It's Tara."

Not Aunt Nicole. How do I feel about this? I'm not sure. Tara's okay. She's been really nice, but I don't know if it's because she actually likes me or if she's just nice to everyone, like her mom is.

"I'm not going to come in and I don't want to bother you, but I know Mom's scared. Are you okay?"

I picture her leaning against the doorframe, her face close to the crack. If I was nicer, I'd let her in, but overreacting makes me feel stupid, and I'd rather not face that stupidity any more than I have to.

My mouth opens three times before anything comes out. "Okay."

"And…" She sounds so hesitant. "I'm sorry for even asking this… Crap. So, um, you're not going to hurt yourself, are you?"

Her words hit hard, making me cringe in embarrassment. This is something I'm asked once in a while. Kids who have gone through similar stuff as I did have a much higher rate of suicide than normal. There were a few times when I didn't care as much if I lived or died. But that's different than wanting to do it to yourself. Isn't it?

"Joy?"

"Just want to be alone. It's the smell." This probably kicks me up another notch on the scale of crazy—kind of sucks to be on the scale at all. My chest feels heavy and I'm embarrassed again.

"The smell?"

"The beer."

"Oh." There's a pause. "Sorry."

I let myself lie back on the floor. This is okay. I can be in here and be okay. The embarrassment and fear are starting to disappear into the floor.

"I'll see you in the morning for school," she says.

Talking through the door seems sort of silly, juvenile in some way. I don't answer.

The floor is scratchy, but the carpet is thick. I pull my knees up, resting my hands on my stomach and breathe. The slow breaths that Lydia makes me practice to keep away panic attacks. It doesn't really work, but it does help calm me when I'm not on the verge of panic, and it passes the time.

I listen to all of the talking and shuffling that happens around bedtime. The house is quiet except for my stomach, which rumbles from neglect.

My body aches when I stand from being on the floor for so long. I'm grateful that everyone in this house has to be up early. It means that the late nights are dark, quiet, and peaceful. I walk softly down the carpeted stairs and into the kitchen. It's all dark. I don't mind being in the dark. There's safety in the darkness—I can disappear. In two minutes I have a peanut butter and jelly sandwich. I grab an apple and take my dinner into the dining room. Maybe if I practice sitting in here with no family, it'll be easier when they're all here.

"Joy?" Uncle Rob's voice is a whisper.

A small sound escapes my throat and fear weakens me. I'm frozen—arms tensed against my sides, and legs stuck to the floor.

"I just wanted you to know I was in here." His voice drops even softer. "Sorry. I was just thinking. I can do that anywhere. I'm leaving." He stands up at the opposite end of the room and starts to move.

My breathing slows down. Slowly. "You shouldn't have to leave for me. It's your house."

I just *spoke* to him.

"It's your house too." He stands silent in the other doorway. "I'm going up to bed. I'm…um…night."

"Night."

I said something else. My heart's hitting hard, and my breathing definitely doesn't fall on the normal scale, but I talked to my uncle. Three months. It took me three months to talk to my own uncle. Guess he shouldn't feel *too* left out. It took me a month before I really spoke with anyone aside from Aunt Nicole.

He stands and watches me for another moment. His face looks... heavy or something. He opens his mouth like he's going to talk, but he backs away and leaves the room.

Relief weakens my knees now that he's gone. I sit in the room by myself, but my heart still won't slow and I'm not sure what to do. As hungry as I was when I got here, my appetite sort of left with Uncle Rob. For a few more minutes, I sit at the table and then get up to throw my sandwich in the trash before going back to my room.

People are coming over. I'm hiding. Maybe she won't notice I'm gone. Maybe she's had just enough to drink to not know I went away. I'm eleven. I'm shaking as the voices get louder. Almost everyone who knows Mom thinks I only visit her sometimes. Do their kids stay inside their houses like me? This can't be normal. None of the kids in the books I read have burns across their backs and have to hide in their rooms. What's wrong with me?

"Joy!" Mom's screech. "Joy!" Mom's screech again. My fists clench the sleeping bag. My eyes squeeze tight. My heart bangs in my ears. No breathing, that'll make it quiet. That'll make this disappear. "JOY!"

I sit bold upright in bed. Another dream. Will they ever stop?

A soft knock on my door. "Joy?" Aunt Nicole's quiet voice. "It's time for school."

I'm finally able to take a deep breath. "Thanks." Now I get to spend another day half-hiding and half-pretending I'm not as crazy as I am.

FIVE
ON ASSIGNMENT

Lydia thinks or "feels" that I'm not aware of my forward progress. So I'm writing again. Homework for her on top of homework from school.

I resist the urge to stick out my tongue even though I'm alone because I'm feeling petulant. But once I start writing, I'm pulled directly back into that day.

My first day at school felt like swimming through a crowded fish tank. I remember so clearly how I tried to keep my hands tucked into my sides. My books clutched in front of me. Over and over, I questioned whether or not I should have come. It's that I already knew I didn't act like Tara and Trent, so anything I could do to fit in I wanted to try.

I hated that I'd wanted this. As I sat through class after class, wishing to pay attention but mostly wanting to disappear.

I wondered about my sanity. The only reason school felt okay was that I wasn't being singled out. I'd been with the Mooresons for two months. I should have known how to be normal at school.

I should know *now* how to be normal at school. Though, it's better. Way better. I sketch in the margins. I used to have notebooks filled with sketches—one of the few things that used to keep me busy during my days at Mom's. I stop as another flood of memories of that home tries to find its way in, and I start writing about school again.

School is easier now, I guess. Nibbling on one small piece of lunch is enough to get me through the rest of the day. Not being able to eat in front of people is something I can't explain so I try not to think about it too much. Tara feels comfortable to be around and always finds me for lunchtime. I can breathe in my classes and I can listen to the teacher enough to sort of know what's happening. The building doesn't feel foreign anymore. I don't love how many people there are. I don't love how enormous the spaces are. I'm grateful every day that I don't have PE.

I know it's easier than my first day. That makes me feel like in another month it'll be even better. I hope.

SIX

SERIOUSLY, AM I MOVING BACKWARD?

We're all in a group session with Lydia. My whole extended family. And it's about as awesome as it sounds. Mostly it's just one more way I'm messing with their lives and another thing that weighs me down with guilt.

"Why don't you like these?" Lydia asks me. "Our group chats. I'd think it would be perfect for you because you're not the focus."

"Because everyone has to be here." How is that not the most obvious thing in the world?

"Do you not want them here?" she asks.

"It's not that I don't want them here." I shake my head. I can't believe she's asking me these questions in front of them.

"You know I'm going to ask you what the problem is."

I'm not looking at her, but I can picture her now. She has on her serious face.

I don't want to see it so I look at my hands clasped together on my lap and let my hair hide my face. "It's that they already had to adjust their lives, and this just sort of adds to the pile of adjustments."

Tara leans forward to look at me through my blanket of hair. "It's totally fine."

I catch Trent's smirk out of the corner of my eye. To me it says he might mind a little bit. He flips his phone over and over. No way he wants to be here.

These sessions are the only times I sit in a chair. If I were on the couch for family days, I'd be pressed against someone else.

Lydia talks to Trent and Tara. I don't hear what they discuss. I'm not into it. I'm just tired.

"Joy?" Lydia's voice again.

"What?" I lift my face just enough to see her through my hair.

"Do you want to tell them the two things I asked you to do?"

"No." One of them involves talking to Uncle Rob. I only sort of did that.

There's silence. Perfect. They're waiting for me.

I let out a loud sigh. One that I hope says I'm not happy about doing this.

"One thing was that I was supposed to talk to someone from my school. I let him walk with me and then talked to him later."

Having to share this with everyone sort of ruins my proud moment. It's such a lame thing to be excited about.

"And the other?"

"I wrote about going to school."

Lydia frowns. This isn't the assignment she was referring to.

I pray she doesn't say anything. I don't want to hurt Uncle Rob's feelings. He seems like a really nice guy. It would suck if he knew that he's on my list of crazy.

"Maybe this week? It's your birthday this week," she prompts.

I nod.

"Sixteen." Aunt Nicole smiles. "We want to do something special but don't want you to feel uncomfortable."

"Then let's just not do anything. Is that okay?" I tilt my head to look at Aunt Nicole. I don't want a party or anything. My birthday in the past was simply an excuse for Mom to invite people over for a party. A Mom-party was never a kid-appropriate party. I remember two years that she forgot my birthday. Those are still my two favorite birthdays. The house was quiet, and I didn't have to wish to disappear after her friends drank too much.

"Well, maybe we could concede and do something *small*? Just our family?" Her voice sounds so...*hopeful*.

"I still..." *can't eat in the same room.* But I keep that to myself.

I feel Lydia's eyes on me. "Joy, what if you let them just do cake? Maybe that would be something you could manage. And then you could try to think about something else you'd like to do with them, maybe later on." She takes a relaxing breath. It's fabulous that *someone* in here is relaxed. Though Trent's lounging on the end of the couch and sort of staring off into space, so maybe he is too.

"A movie?" Maybe we could watch a movie and then I could eat my cake and not feel like they're looking at me.

"Would you like to go *out* to a movie?" Aunt Nicole's hopeful voice is back.

"Oh..." I shake my head. "No..." No way. What's wrong with me? We're talking about going to the movies. People do it all the time. I just don't want to sit next to anyone. It seems sort of impossible. It also seems impossible to ignore how many people would be there. Going to a movie and staring at the floor like I do in school sort of defeats the purpose.

The room is silent for a moment. "I'm sorry." My eyes are filling with tears. "I'm so..." *broken.*

"You don't have to be sorry, Joy." Lydia's shaking her head.

"I'd still rather pretend my birthday doesn't exist." I concentrate on letting my breath out slowly, hoping to hold in my tears.

"Tara and Trent, why don't you two step outside and I'll send the rest of the family out in a minute," Lydia says.

Trent swings his tall body up and shuffles toward the door. Tara stands up behind him. She gives me a small wave as she passes.

"Why do we have to drag them in here?" I ask as the door closes behind them. "I'm sure they don't like it."

"And I know how you feel about it." Lydia looks at me over her notebook with a half smile. "They're only here sometimes, and it's important for them to have some understanding of how difficult things can be for you."

I start to say something else, but Uncle Rob's still in the room, and I'm not sure how much I'm ready to talk around him. I clamp my mouth shut.

"How are you two doing?" Lydia asks.

I know without taking my eyes off my lap that she's talking to Uncle Rob.

"Well, I'm sure when Joy and I can chat a bit, we'll have a lot in common," he says. "She plows through her homework the way I used to." His voice is soft and kind. "We exchanged a few words the other night."

Now I'm glad Lydia will know I did both things on my list without me bringing it up again.

Uncle Rob sounds so nice, but even now I can't bring myself to look at him. Deep voices still hit me in places I don't want to think about.

"Well, Joy and I need a few minutes alone, and then I'll let you all go."

Aunt Nicole and Uncle Rob stand up and walk out. I finally relax into the chair.

"I got your email about talking to the boy at school," Lydia says to me. "That's pretty cool. And school. You know I was against you starting up, but you're surviving it. Your letter to me about the difference between now and when you started was great. I hope the assignment made it more obvious to you how much things are going in a good direction."

"Thanks." My eyes find hers for the first time today.

"I don't have to ask why Rob scares you."

I'm silent and try not to think about the same thing, but I can almost feel the rough hands on my waist, the knife against my neck, the whispered threats. I suck in a breath and press my fingers on the bridge of my nose as my body starts to shake.

"Joy. Look at me."

The stubble down my neck, the slice of pain when I whimpered and the knife dug in farther.

Lydia moves and her hand gently touches my wrist, making me jump. "Where were you?"

"The last place I want to be."

She smiles softly. "Keep your eyes on me for a moment, okay?"

I do because I like Lydia's round face and bright smile, and I know it'll keep me in the here and now.

"What brought you back there?"

"Uncle Rob. When you said…" I trail off, knowing she'll know.

"I can see your breathing already slowing back down." Her voice is mellow, quiet, and calm. "Remember shutting your eyes makes it worse. Try to force them open. To take in your surroundings when you find yourself there again, okay?"

I nod and swallow, trying to push away the fear, but its grip on me is solid.

"When I talk to your aunt and uncle without you, I can tell the love they have for you is the real thing. I want you to remember that. We can hold off on talking to Rob. Okay?"

My shoulders relax in relief, and they ache—a sign I'm even tenser today than normal. "Okay."

"And I'll let your aunt know that you should get the backseat to yourself on the drive home. Would that help?"

I nod, grateful, relieved, and feeling like I should be able to handle sharing a car with Uncle Rob. But in this moment, I care a lot more about having a seat to myself than how well I'm doing with the family.

"Your goal this week is to have cake and enjoy the movie, all right?"

"Fine." I let out a long breath. At least this goal feels possible.

"I'm just torturing you here, aren't I?" She chuckles. "No writing assignments this week. I promise."

"Okay." But now I make sure our eyes don't connect—sometimes it's just easier to avoid her hopes for me that way. She doesn't understand that I don't know how to move forward the way she wants me to.

"It's because I know that you, more than a lot of girls I see, have a chance at a really amazing life," she says. "You're smart. I know you're worried about being afraid of people right now. But the girls who come in here and freely talk about things and are okay out in social settings after an ordeal like yours, do all right but not as well as someone like you can. They're the ones that *seem* okay when they really aren't. You're going to start breaking free from this, Joy, and when you do, life's going to be good to you."

The thing is, she has no idea if life will be good to me or not. None. A lot of my life still depends on the people around me and I have no idea how to be around them. Or even if I want to be. Learning how to feel normal is a hard thing to believe in.

"Please, just cake, no singing." I wasn't able to eat a bite of dinner because I was anxious about this very thing.

The problem is that I know Aunt Nicole worked hard on my cake today. I know Tara helped her decorate it. And I know they're all here for me. So guilt over all of this holds me here. I'm trapped.

"Nobody likes the singing." Trent laughs. "You can suffer with the rest of us."

"Trent." Aunt Nicole shakes her head.

"I just think everyone's being a little too careful. That's all." He shrugs.

At least I don't have to wonder if he's sparing my feelings.

They sing happy birthday to me. I force my eyes to stay open, because if I let them close, I'd see a different set of people. I wish for the floor to swallow me whole.

My shoulder rests against the wall as I watch *Pirates of the Caribbean*. Uncle Rob and Trent keep commenting on how awesome the picture is on the new TV. A flat, black monstrosity attached to the wall. I've never seen this movie, but Trent and Uncle Rob swear it's one of the best movies of all time.

I still can't bring myself to eat my cake. It looks so good, and it's just sitting on my plate. Everyone else has finished theirs. Uncle Rob and Tara even had seconds. Not me. Eating is such a stupid thing to have a problem with. Who gets weirded out about eating in front of people? It shouldn't be a big deal. I mean, logically I *know* it shouldn't be a big deal. People do it all the time. At home, at restaurants, at school.

I slide a bite off the pile of chocolate with my fork. Now I just have to get it to my mouth. Easy. Everyone's watching the movie. The scene is intense. The music is intense. My timing is perfect. I take the bite and it's as good as it smells. I let the chocolate flavor fill my mouth when I suddenly feel watched. Everything in me stops. Trent's staring.

It takes all the self-control I have not to spit out the cake. My stomach clenches up. I set my plate on the floor, lean against the wall, and return my eyes to the screen. Maybe I'll eat some later.

I'm lying in my white bed, staring at the blank ceiling. I had one bite of cake. The rest is downstairs. I may wait until I think everyone's asleep. Or I could pack myself some in my lunch tomorrow and then find somewhere to hide at school so I can eat it.

"Trent." Uncle Rob's voice carries through the walls. Even his quiet one. "I know you're just trying to be yourself here, and I'm glad, but..."

"Sorry, I just feel like we could shake it out of her and she'd start hanging out with us like normal." Trent's voice is full of frustration.

"You don't understand." His voice is so smooth, warm. "She didn't have a normal. Her mom kept her inside almost all the time. She didn't go out. She didn't go to school. She suffered the kinds of abuse you can't even imagine. All the literature we were given to help her out was stuff that has to do with kids raised in cults. This is how much of an adjustment she's going through."

"What happened to her?" he asks.

"My guess is that if you can imagine it, she probably went

through it. What's important now is for you and all of us to have some patience and understanding and know that the best thing to do is be friendly and not push her to do things she's not comfortable with."

"Okay." But Trent's voice makes it sound like it isn't okay. Like he's just playing along because he has to.

"Night, Trent."

"Night, Dad."

I don't know about what he said, about imagining things…I can imagine some pretty bad things. Some things that didn't happen to me. I don't want to think about the things that did, but now they're running through my head.

The laughing at the beginning of the evenings. That's when I'd get an occasional cigarette put out on my back. But later in the evening? That's when I'd close the door to my room and hope they'd forget I was there—it only worked sometimes.

And the day after something like that was always a time to be quiet. Silent. I'd sit in my room and read and reread all the schoolbooks that came to me in the mail for home school. By the end of the year I'd read everything many times. There was no other way to get books. Not that I knew of.

Now that I'm not at Mom's anymore, I'm sort of in awe I survived it all. The thought of someone walking into my room now the way it happened then—now that I know what life is like without all of that—the thought staggers me.

I just want to go to sleep, but there's no way that's happening tonight. The pictures come again and again. Mom's cackling laugh, the one that meant she's oblivious to what's going on. The last boyfriend, Richard, was the worst—beer belly, smelly, his stubble scratched my face and any other place he'd see fit to have his mouth. He was the one with the knife. Just to make sure I'd be quiet. He didn't know I already had lots of practice.

My body starts to shake, and I roll into a ball as the tears begin. *I'm safe. I'm with family. I'm safe. I'm safe. I'm safe.*

But no matter what my surroundings are, I don't feel safe. Ever. It's even worse, because what I feel doesn't mix with logic. My body continues to shake and my tears keep dropping onto the sheets.

My pillow is soaked. How long has it been? Seconds? Minutes? Hours?

"Joy?" I hear Aunt Nicole's voice and soft knocking on my door.

"Yeah?" I rub my face frantically a few times, pushing off any wetness.

"Can I come in?"

"Yeah." But I don't want to talk. The walls in this house are made of paper.

She walks slowly into my room. She's in one of Uncle Rob's T-shirts and sweatpants she probably just threw on. I think it's sort of sweet that she sleeps in his shirts. "Do you want to take something?" Her voice is a near-silent whisper. "It's past midnight."

I roll onto my back. I'm so *weak*. Instead of answering, I just nod. Xanax—the nighttime snack of losers. Perfect. At least I won't relive anything more tonight. No dreams. Just sleep.

SEVEN

WAIT. IS THIS WHAT IT'S LIKE TO DO BETTER?

The house is quiet when I step downstairs after finishing homework, and it reminds me of my home before this one.

In the trailer, I'd wait until everything was this quiet and then I would do the dishes and sweep the floor and take out the trash. I learned quickly to do those things nearly silently. I had most of the night, so time wasn't a problem. Sometimes I could clean during the day when Mom was gone, but I never knew when she would be back.

At the Mooresons', everything is clean when the family goes to bed. Aunt Nicole cleans after her whirlwind morning routine, and Uncle Rob cleans up after dinner. I'm not sure how to help. I should be helping.

I wander into the kitchen where Aunt Nicole stands sifting through her phone with an exasperated look on her face.

"You okay?" I ask quietly.

"I haven't been able to find time to schedule a hair appointment."

Yeah. Because she spends so much time taking me to my appointments.

"I'm trying to find a time that works for both me and my hairdresser. It's not going well."

"I can do it," I say so fast that my words topple over each other.

Aunt Nicole rests her phone on the counter and her eyes meet mine. "What?"

"I know how to cut hair. Mom cut hair. I know how." I hope. I did some of the neighbors and the neighbors' kids. Sometimes. Mom liked the extra money.

Aunt Nicole is quiet for so long that I'm wondering if I've really messed up. I'm never sure if I'm doing or saying the right thing.

"Stay right there." She smiles and points. "This is perfect."

In less than two minutes, Aunt Nicole has a stool set up next to the sink, a towel wrapped around her shoulders, a spray bottle of water and one of conditioner, and I'm holding scissors and a comb. I actually start to relax now that I have a task. As I take in the shape of her face, I realize her hair's all wrong. "Do you trust me?" I ask.

Aunt Nicole raises a brow. "Anything you want. I've had the same hair for years."

I spray her hair and start cutting. A *lot*.

"You're doing Mom's hair?" Tara's smile is wide as she pauses against the counter. I love the days when Trent and his dad aren't here—the house feels so much more relaxed. "Can you do me when you're done?" Tara's sweetness practically pours out of everything she says, making her an easy person for me to be around.

"If you want." Does she know I'd love to, but that I'm not sure how to use those words or if I should?

"Awesome," she says.

I cut until Aunt Nicole's hair rests just under her ears.

Tara claps. "This is so cool!"

Now I'm smiling. I can't help it. I'm extra careful with shaping the cut just right, keeping the front slightly longer than the back and adding layers so her hair sits the way I imagined.

"Oh my gosh, Mom!" Tara grins. "It's so *awesome.*"

Aunt Nicole runs her hands through the layers a few times. "This feels so strange." Her smile is wide. "But I think I'm going to love it."

"Nicole?" Uncle Rob stops in the doorway, smiling. "You look amazing."

"Thank you, Joy." Aunt Nicole stands and gives me a small hug, but I step away after a brief moment. The closeness is still intense.

I back to the other side of the kitchen, just in case Uncle Rob decides to come all the way in. "Don't thank me until you see it yourself," I whisper.

Now that Uncle Rob's here, I lower my voice. Like maybe he won't notice me in the room, which is silly because there's only four of us in here. My wish to not be noticed is just something else that belongs on my list.

"Me next." Tara sits. "If you're up to it."

I stand unsure. I *can* cut her hair. I want to, just not if her dad's going to be in the room. I know him being here shouldn't matter, but just like always, it does matter.

"I'm taking your mother out to dinner," Uncle Rob says. His eyes don't leave her face as he brings her hand up for a kiss.

He's so different than any man I've ever been around—quiet and gentle. I don't understand him.

"You guys can order pizza. Here's forty bucks." He sets it on the counter. "Nice job, Joy. You're very talented."

I don't look at him because I'm completely pathetic, but I manage a nod. I do a lot of that around here.

Uncle Rob wraps his arm around his wife and they're gone.

"So," Tara says. "I want something funky. And something that will hide my fat cheeks."

I shake my head. "You don't have fat cheeks." That's crazy. She's not fat. She's soft. She has this small waist but a real shape to her. I'm jealous of how her body curves so smoothly.

"You're only saying that because you're so thin." She points at me.

"I'm too skinny. I look sick or something." I hate my bony body. "I envy your soft cheeks. I can't imagine mine ever looking like yours. You're so pretty."

Tara's jaw drops. "You are like the sweetest person ever."

I don't know how to react to her words so I pick up my scissors instead. "How about we make it a little shorter, just under your shoulders, and add layers everywhere?" I can see her new look in my head and want to get started.

"Sounds awesome."

I shift my raincoat hood farther over my face, enjoying my walk home from school even though it's raining. My feet are damp and cold, but it feels good to be away from hot, dry, and dusty of California.

"It's my walking buddy."

I snap my head around.

Justin.

Now is when I should speak, right? He's not bad. He's just a guy. A guy who goes to my school. Logically this is all cool. I just need to convince my body of this. Deep breath in. I'm okay. We're okay. This is okay.

"Don't look so surprised." He chuckles. "We're both walking from the same place to homes that are close to each other."

"Sorry." That's a word I'm good at, and I think my voice even sounded all right. He doesn't know me well enough to hear the shakiness. I hate that my nerves are on edge just because he's close.

He moves in step next to me. "Is this okay? I mean, is it okay if we walk together?"

I nod. That's something else I'm pretty great at. Nodding.

I like Justin's shoes. They used to be white, but he's drawn all over them so there's barely any white left. Makes me wonder if he gets in trouble for violating dress code. "That's really cool." I point down.

Drawing. I suddenly miss drawing so much I only half understand why I stopped. All my sketchbooks were taken as evidence like most of my stuff from home, but I wouldn't want those anyway. I'd want new ones. If…If I can still find it inside me to draw. Might have to add it to my list.

○ *Can't talk to people.*
○ *Hides in her room.*
○ *Can't stand the smell of cigarettes and beer.*
○ *Is afraid of her own uncle for no particular reason.*
○ *Isn't sure she can draw*

"What's cool?" he asks.

"Your shoes." Now I feel good. I'm talking to someone I don't know. A guy. A guy that's not my cousin. A guy I find pretty cute. And I like his drawings. Maybe I'll start to do some of my own again. Maybe. Then I can start crossing some of the crazy off my list.

"Hey, thanks. My dad hates them. He keeps giving me a hard time for making him buy shoes that I destroy." He kicks a stray rock off the sidewalk. "But drawing helps with the ADD, so I keep drawing."

"Oh."

"How's the breathing today?"

"Fine." Right. He thinks I have asthma. I'll need to straighten that out. But not today. Today I'm just trying to breathe and concentrate on our shoes on the pavement. And not panic.

"You're a girl of few words."

"Yep."

He laughs.

Was that funny? "I like to listen."

My head is silent. My heart is silent. I just gave him a piece of me. A piece of truth.

° *Spoke with a boy. With Justin. Didn't lie and didn't have a panic attack. Yet.*

But I won't tell Lydia about my drawings. She doesn't know how much I love art, and it would just end up on the list of things she asks me to work on. That part of me I want to get back on my own.

"Cool," he says. We walk a few steps in silence. "I like to talk."

I let myself steal a glance at him.

"There you are." A crooked smile pulls up one corner of his mouth.

I smile back. I'm so brave! Well, brave for me.

"I'm not bugging you, am I?"

"No." Wow. I like walking next to him. I want him to keep talking about things, anything. What will he talk about next? What kinds of things does he think about? What does he do outside of school? Most kids have after-school hobbies or clubs and stuff, just not me, not right now. Not yet.

Wow. *Not yet.* But I will, I think. I'll start to be able to have things after school. Maybe something I do. Something I like or something I'm good at. All these ideas and thoughts leave me with the most amazing feeling. *Hope.*

"Well, I'll be seeing you around," Justin says.

What? Is he leaving? My heart sinks as I come to a stop. Oh. I'm at the house. He's walking backward, still looking at me. I'm kind of sad our time today is over, but maybe we can talk in Government or something. I wave and turn up the driveway still clinging to the faint feeling of hope that I'm starting to belong.

EIGHT

SOMETIMES THERE ARE NO GOOD ANSWERS

Aunt Nicole and I sit in Lydia's office.

"I've come here without you a few times," Aunt Nicole says.

My heart jumps. Am I in trouble? Why are they talking about me without me?

"Relax, Joy." Aunt Nicole rests her hand on my shoulder and I flinch.

I hear her suck in a breath.

"Okay, Joy?" Lydia's voice. "I need you to look at me, please."

I do as asked.

"You and your aunt are okay, right?"

"Yeah."

"Why did you jump away from her?"

I'm so stupid. When will I get enough control over my body to stop overreacting? "I didn't mean to. It just…happens."

"You feel stressed?"

"A little. I didn't know she was here talking about me without me." That's understandable, right?

Aunt Nicole turns on the couch to face me. "I was here for me. Because I feel like I should have rescued you a long time ago."

"Rescued?" It sounds so dramatic.

"Yes." She nods. Her eyes are intent on my face. "I play that brief phone call over and over in my head. When you were eight. I knew you weren't in school, and I was worried, but you were such a long drive away."

"And you and Mom don't get along." It never seemed weird that my aunt didn't visit. Mom doesn't like her.

"I called child services after we talked."

"You did?"

"They said they came to the house and everything seemed fine."

I lean back against the couch feeling weak. I remember. I haven't remembered that in forever. After my call with Aunt Nicole, Mom and I talked about school. She told me that people might be coming over and warned me that if they thought we didn't get along, I might go somewhere else. We had so much fun over the next few days. We read together and watched TV and cleaned our small home. When child services popped in for their surprise visit we were ready.

I was so afraid that Mom would go back to how she was or that we'd be separated when we were finally having fun. I was very convincing when I told them how well Mom and I did and that the conversation with my aunt was all a misunderstanding. We never see her. How could she know?

My eyes close. After those people left, everything went back to how it was before. Mom's drinking even got worse for a while when she split with the nice guy who helped set me up with school.

"She only pretended so they wouldn't take me," I say. "Or maybe so they wouldn't take her. I think she wanted me there, but I have no idea why." Why? Why? That horrible question again. The question with no good answers, the one that needs to be stuffed away. There's no good explanation for anything that's happened in my life, the good or bad. I won't open my eyes, not now. I don't even try to stop the memories. Today I know I'll lose.

Mom's smiling face comes up first, our old brown flowered couch behind her. Then I see her smoker's teeth. She yells. I hear her harsh voice like I'm there. "I don't believe you, Joy! Something's going on!" She hated how much attention Richard gave me, but there's no way she hated it as much as I did.

Aunt Nicole slides next to me. "I can't imagine why anyone wouldn't want you. You're an angel, Joy."

I shake my head. Her voice fades the memory away and all I see is black.

"Rob and I. We have a good life and we didn't see it. We weren't seeing how lucky we all were. I mean, we get along okay, but learning about you, and having you in our house...we appreciate all the smaller things more than we ever have."

"Because my life was so sucky?" I feel an actual smile start to form.

"And because you're so special."

My eyes squeeze tighter.

"Open your eyes, Joy," Lydia says. "We both know that helps."

"I have felt so often like I completely failed you," Aunt Nicole says.

"How could you think that?" I ask. Now my eyes have to open. I stare at Aunt Nicole's round face, her newly shortened hair.

"Because if I had been more persistent, if I'd pushed visits. I just feel like...maybe I would have been able to get you out of there sooner."

I shrug. "I never thought about you not being there sooner. I'm still sort of overwhelmed by what you're doing for me now." And I don't want them being nice to me because of guilt.

"We love having you at our house. I need you to know that."

I stare. What words could say thank you in the right way?

Lydia leans forward in her chair. "Joy, you have to know your Uncle Rob feels the same. The only reason he isn't here is because I know how hard it is for you to talk around him."

"I'll work on it." I'm promising myself. I'm more determined.

Lydia leans toward me. "Maybe just try to spend some time in the same room as him, okay? Small steps. Don't feel bad about taking small steps."

Right. Baby steps. One tiny step after another. Maybe when I'm eighty I'll really start to get somewhere.

Uncle Rob is in the living room reading a book near the gas fire. Fake fire, only it's real because it can still burn things. Sort of funny.

So, small steps. I don't want to be crazy forever. I don't want to keep being afraid of the people who live in this house. It's supposed to be my house too, even if it doesn't always feel like it.

And I don't want to be afraid of the kids at school. Like Justin. This house seems like a safe place to start. But being in the same room as Uncle Rob still feels like a pretty big step.

I sit on the floor near the blue flames and pull out my math homework. There. We're in the same room. This is good. He's reading. I'm working. Seems perfect. I take a barrette out of my bag and pull the hair off my face. It's something I don't normally do because most of the time I'm trying to hide.

He glances over his book, probably as unsure about me being in here as I am. Maybe he just doesn't like me. Maybe that's why we don't talk. Or maybe he read something in my file that makes him leave me alone—there are certainly enough instances that would make him wonder if I'd ever want to be around men. Or maybe there are things in there that would make him not want to be around *me*.

"Hi," I whisper.

His smile is big and immediate. "Hi, Joy. Glad you joined me." His voice is quiet but he's not whispering.

It's hot in front of the fire and the warmth is a nice contrast to the wet day. Now that I'm here, I don't want to move. I spread out my math book and notebook in front me. The heat is too much for all the layers I have on, so I slide my sweatshirt off, and lie on my stomach in my tank top. The warmth feels even better on my bare skin. I rest my chin on my palms and my elbows on the floor. After not paying attention in math, I'm trying to figure out parabolas using the examples from the text. I think I'm getting it. When I flip the page, Uncle Rob sucks in a breath behind me.

I turn to look at him. "Are you okay?" I ask.

"Are *you?*" His forehead is wrinkled up, and I swear I see tears in his eyes. What happened?

"I'm just working on parabolas. I didn't pay attention in class so…" But we're so not talking about this. What are we talking about then? I sit up to face him. What could be wrong?

He's staring at my bare scarred shoulders and back. Right. Tank top. How did I miss that?

"Your back and shoulders…All those round, white…I'm sorry, you don't want…" He shakes his head and leans back in his chair, still watching me.

"You have my file. I figured you and Aunt Nicole knew everything." How could he be surprised by the scars? All the details are in there, exposing me in a way I didn't ask for.

"No." His eyes meet mine. His voice is still so quiet. He doesn't look at me the way the men mom brought home did. Not at all.

"We asked for information on what we should and shouldn't do with and for you. We only wanted to know what we needed to. The rest is yours, personal."

What? I assumed they'd read everything available to them. They invited me into their house, to be around their kids. I'd think they'd want all the details.

"It's scars from cigarette burns," I explain.

His lips press together and his chin quivers like he's fighting not to cry.

I need to make him feel better. "They're no big deal." Any

scarring you can see isn't a big deal. All the other stuff, the stuff you can't see, that's what weighs me down.

Tears roll down his cheeks. "There's so *many*."

He's crying. Uncle Rob is crying because of me. Over things that happened what feels like a lifetime ago.

"They didn't all happen at once." And now we're talking. Uncle Rob and I, and I'm not terrified. That alone feels like progress.

He's leaning forward in his chair again, book forgotten. "Joy... No one. No one should ever..."

I don't want him to be so sad over me. I'm fighting for something to say. "It looks a lot worse than it is, Uncle Rob. Stuff like that only happened when everyone was drinking and having fun. It wasn't..." I shake my head. "It wasn't like you're thinking."

He's still silent and he's wiped his tears once, but they're still there.

"It's not like they held me down and..." But I can't think about being held down. That pulls me into a worse place than where Uncle Rob is right now. "I'm sorry, I'll go."

"No, Joy. I'm sorry. It took me by surprise, that's all. I don't want you to go—if you're okay staying in here with me." Uncle Rob's eyes that hold so much kindness.

"I'll be right back." I go to my room and dig around for a T-shirt. Something that covers my scars. When I step back into the small den, his tears have dried and he has his book in his hand.

There's an almost apologetic frown on his face when I sit in front of the fire. He probably feels bad that I changed for him.

"I'm really glad you decided to come stay with us," he says.

As opposed to all my other options. "Thanks." I look at him for just another second. "I'm back to parabolas."

"Let me know if you need any help." He leans back behind his book.

"I will, thanks."

Uncle Rob and I are suddenly not only talking, but I shared a bit of my past with him. Maybe there will be a point when I feel like I belong here. Maybe.

NINE
MORE LISTS

I look down the list of reasons why I'm crazy. This list I keep in the back of my notebook, not in the front.

Can't talk to people. But I'm totally getting better. I poise my pen to cross it out, but I can't. Not quite yet.

- *Hides in her room.*
- *Can't function around the smell of cigarettes or beer.*
- *Is afraid of her own uncle for no particular reason.*

I sat in the same room with him. I shared a bit of my past with him, and he saw my scars. I didn't freak out *or* have a panic attack. I cross him off the list, and the line through those words signifies so much stress and worry that's now slipped away.

Oh, wait. Panicking. That needs to be added to the list.

- *Has panic attacks—set off by stupid things.*

Okay, so one thing crossed off, one thing added.

These are not good stats.

I'm in the house alone, which rarely happens. Tara's staying after school, and Trent's hanging out with friends. I pull out the lunch I didn't eat in the cafeteria today and sit in the kitchen.

I hear the front door open and my body tenses up. Who is it?

A girl giggles. "Are you sure?"

"Yeah, just my cousin's here and she practically lives in her room." Trent.

"Okay."

I'm listening closely so I know where they are in the house and where I shouldn't be. What are they doing? Why does Trent want time alone with her? Why do these questions make my body shake?

"I really wanted to kiss you again," Trent says.

The house is silent for a few moments.

"Follow me," he whispers. Their shoes drop to the floor, and I think he's taken her into the den.

I'm trapped. There's no way to go upstairs without passing that room, and I really don't want to pass that room. What are they doing? Is he kissing her again? Are they doing more? Will they soon? I leave my lunch on the counter and start to slowly walk up the stairs. Maybe if I'm quiet enough, I'll be invisible too.

I stop when I see Trent and his girlfriend on the floor in front of the fire. They're still in their school uniforms, but he's on top of her, kissing her hard. My stomach knots up. I want to run, but I can't make my feet move. What's wrong with me?

Her arms go around his back, pulling him closer to her. I recognize her. Felicity, I think.

Her face turns to the side and our eyes catch.

I gasp and run up the stairs.

"Hey!" Trent yells. I startled him too. "Make some damn noise, would you? Or toughen up a little and tell me you're here when I come in the door!"

I pull my door closed behind me, breathing hard, and lean against it, as if it will somehow be more closed with my weight.

"My cousin. She's so weird. I'm sorry." Trent.

"She just freaked me out, that's all." Felicity.

"When she's upset she'll stay in there for hours."

Felicity giggles, and I'm sure they pick up where they left off.

Why does it make me sick? No one's forcing me to do what he's doing to her. It doesn't matter if it's happening somewhere else in the house. Well, it *shouldn't* matter, anyway.

This should probably go on my list, but I don't want to add something to that right now. I'm trying to take things off, not put things on.

I put on the yoga pants Aunt Nicole bought for me, and sit on my bed. My backpack's downstairs, which sucks. I can't even get my homework done. But there's no way I'm going down there again.

For the first time, I contemplate taking a Xanax from my aunt's bathroom without talking to her, but I don't. Instead I curl up in my bed. Maybe I could sleep for a bit. I let my eyes fall closed, and drift off.

There are some thuds, bumps, and voices downstairs. Now I hear Aunt Nicole's footsteps. Hers are light, like Tara's, but she moves faster than Tara.

"Joy?"

I'm silent. I don't want to talk, to explain. I just want to sleep.

"Joy, I know your room is your room, but I'm worried about you so I'm going to open the door." She cracks the door and peers in.

"Just come in." I'd rather have her in here than talking in the hallway where everyone can hear.

"Why are you up here?" Aunt Nicole asks.

"Because I'm tired." That seems safe enough. And I'm always up here. I'm not sure why today is different.

"You left a half-eaten lunch and your backpack downstairs." Her head tilts to the side as she looks at me.

I don't answer. My lunch will lead to more questions.

"Did Trent do something? I think it was just you two here."

I open my mouth once and nothing comes out. I open it again. "No."

Her eyes narrow, just slightly. She doesn't believe me.

The thing is, he really didn't do anything. Just made me uncomfortable, which made me feel stupid. He yelled, but he and Tara yell at each other sometimes.

"Why did you still have your lunch from school?"

I don't answer.

"Joy." She sits on the edge of my bed and I scoot away. "No, Joy. We're past this. Is you eating your lunch after school a normal thing?"

I nod.

"Why?"

I'm stupid. I *feel* stupid. Why do I have to be so worried about everything? All the time? I grab handfuls of blankets and rest my chin on my hands. "I don't know."

The silence hurts—as if there are things unsaid I probably wouldn't want to hear.

"Can I get you anything?"

I shake my head.

"I brought your backpack."

Relief spreads through my shoulders, relaxing me. I have my backpack. My homework. I can do it before everyone goes to sleep.

"I'll bring dinner up, but I'd rather see you downstairs."

"Not tonight, please."

She frowns as she stands up. "Okay. Is there anything else? Can we talk about anything else?"

"No."

A few moments later, the door closes behind her.

I'm on the floor with my backpack in seconds. My math homework waits in the book. My reading for English is also in here. All these things I have control over. I can do them well. And I will.

"I hope you're happy!" Trent's voice carries down the hall. "Joy. I know you're listening. I'm in trouble and no one knows what for. I'm not buying your silent act one bit. It's old and it's tired!" His door slams and I hear Uncle Rob's feet on the stairs.

He doesn't knock on Trent's door, just goes in. I hear low angry voices paired with a few loud outbursts from Trent. I jump each time someone yells.

Perfect. Now Trent will hate me forever. I have to do something to fix this. I can't have Trent hate me. We live together. I force myself off the floor and open my door.

Uncle Rob steps out of Trent's room and our eyes catch.

"He didn't do anything. I promise. I'm still…" *crazy.*

Uncle Rob takes a step toward my room, but I close the door between us and release my breath. I did my part. Now I can hide and not feel guilty. Only I still do.

I'm in the narrow dingy-white hallway of my old house. The smell is the same. There's a man in my room. I can't see in, but I know he's there. Does he know I'm just outside the door? My hand is on the doorknob— when did that happen?

I slowly let go of it, but when I do, the knob clicks back into place. I didn't even realize I was opening the door. I hear movement in my room. Without thinking, I run. It doesn't matter that Mom freaks out when I go near the front door. It doesn't matter. I need to get away.

My legs push hard, only they're so weak. Like I've been tied down for days. Only I've never been tied down for days. Only held down long enough for things I couldn't escape.

His face appears. Richard. My legs push faster. My scream is stuck in my throat. Can I breathe? I try to suck in a breath. The hallway gets longer and longer, my legs get weaker and weaker. His beer breath, stubble, and belly are getting closer.

My body tries another scream. I definitely can't breathe. I'm running, but the hallway won't end. I'm almost to the door. Almost. I reach out. I jerk the door open. I'm free. But then I run straight into Trent who grabs my upper arms.

I find a breath to scream.

The sound rips from my lungs, startling me into sitting.

"Breathe, Joy." Aunt Nicole rests a hand on my knee. I'm not sure when she came in.

I open my mouth to talk, but I have nothing to say.

"Let's flip your pillow over, okay?" she asks.

She always does this. She says it helped her kids when they were little. I let her do it because I know she wants to think she's doing something for me. But I don't know how flipping a pillow over could help with dreams.

I lie down to show her I'm okay. Even though I have no idea if I'm okay or not.

TEN
BETTER?

I reach for the front door to start my walk to school. I'm not going in the car because after yesterday and last night I'd rather not ride with Trent.

"Joy, wait. Trent wants to talk to you," Aunt Nicole says from the kitchen.

In my limited experience, if Trent wanted to talk to me, Trent would be the one talking right now. Not his mom.

"I'm walking today. It's no big deal."

"Joy." Her voice is stern. Up until this moment, Aunt Nicole's pretty much let me do whatever I want. Mostly because I don't do anything. But I can tell by her tone this is different.

I shuffle into the kitchen.

She glares at Trent.

Trent's eyes shift to mine. "Sorry if I made you uncomfortable. It's not a problem giving you a ride to school."

I stand and stare, having no idea what I should do.

Aunt Nicole's eyes are on me next.

Right. Okay. I need to say something.

"Thanks. I like to walk, though." My eyes float to Aunt Nicole's expectant face, Trent's annoyed one, and then to Tara's.

Tara gives me a grimace and a shrug of apology. "I'll walk with you, today." She steps around me, and I follow her out the door.

"Well, that was awkward," Tara says when we reach the end of the driveway.

I nod in agreement.

"Sorry about Trent. He's gotten worse this year. Thinks he's some big stud or something." I can tell without looking that she's rolling her eyes.

I don't say anything.

"Does it bother you when I talk? Would you rather it just be quiet?" she asks.

"I like you talking." Is that a good enough explanation? I find Tara interesting, and there's nothing I want to say.

"So, last year Trent dated this awesome girl named Caitlynn. We all adored her. They split just before this year, and he's sort of become…I don't know, but he's already gone through a couple girls. This girl, Kia, and I used to be really good friends, but now she's hanging with the same crowd as Trent, and, I mean, I like to go out once in a while, but it's like they can't get enough."

Tara continues to talk. I soak her words up and realize that she's not having the best senior year. The tone of her voice is upbeat, but

I can tell she's feeling separated from her friends, and her brother is letting it all happen.

Even though her problems are completely different than mine, I actually take comfort in the knowledge that even when someone's life looks pretty perfect, it really isn't.

We're watching a movie in Government, and every time I look up to see if Justin is watching me, he is. Just his eyes make my stomach and chest feel all light and tingly.

I glance over again. This time he isn't looking at me and I take in his features. He has a small bump on his nose, an angled chin, thin lips, and really smooth skin. His nearly black hair is kind of shaggy, and it looks soft. His lashes hit the hair that falls over his forehead. His eyes are kind like Uncle Rob's.

Justin turns and his smile spreads when our eyes meet again.

I look down at my lap. Now I feel bad about the inhaler thing. I've come a long way in a short amount of time, so I want to keep moving forward.

I lied.

I write it on a piece of paper and slip it onto Justin's desk.

His forehead wrinkles up and then he writes quickly, holding the paper out toward me.

About what?

I don't have asthma.

Just writing it makes me feel better because I needed to tell him.

Why would you lie about that?

Because I sometimes have trouble breathing.

Why?

Will the questions never stop coming?

I just…I sometimes think about things and it makes my lungs not work right.

Is that enough?

Like, panic attacks? My mom used to get those.

So, he kind of gets that part of me. And even though my breathing is shallow, I feel like I'm doing something new. That's cool.

Really? I pass the note back.

He's smiling as he writes. That's good. That has to be good.

Yeah. It's pretty common, not that big of a deal, but she'd get them for no reason at all

I'm tons lighter. I mean, tons.

Don't say anything.

He chuckles under his breath as he writes.

How big of a jerk do you think I am?

I don't know yet.

I laugh a little as I send the note back to him. *Laugh.* A real one. Not one designed to make my aunt or cousins feel better, a real, honest laugh.

"Joy?" Our teacher. "Keep quiet back there."

"Sorry." Only I'm totally not sorry because it feels amazing to be talking like this.

Maybe you'd let me take you for a drive or something? So I can show you I'm not a jerk?

His face has softened, and his dark eyes watch me as I read.

He's asking me out. I stare at the paper and then over at him. He's smiling at me. My heart suddenly gets louder. What do I do in a car alone with him? My eyes slide over him again. I can ride in a car with Trent, and Trent's way bigger. But Trent's my cousin, and Justin is not my cousin. I suck in a deep breath.

Maybe.

I hand the paper back over.

His smile falters a little, and I feel the small, subtle movement of disappointment in my chest. I don't want him to feel bad.

He nods, looks at me, and mouths, "Okay." He slumps back in his seat.

Our note-writing is over. I feel almost rejected, like he doesn't want to talk to me anymore. But that's silly, I told him no first. Well, not *no*. *Maybe.* Almost the same thing, right?

"Do you have the car today?" I whisper.

He nods.

"Maybe you could give me a ride home?" I can't believe those words just came out of my mouth. What am I thinking?

His smile is back. "Okay."

I feel my mouth pull into a smile to match his.

This whole situation with Justin makes me feel this huge burst of hope. But then I remember Trent and his girlfriend in the den when he gave her a ride home. Is that what Justin will expect?

Why didn't I think of that before I asked? I can't get in his car if that's what he'll want. Can't.

It's raining hard when school is over, but I have my raincoat, so I'm good. The walk is short. I pull my hood up as I step out of the school.

"You're not trying to ditch me, are you?" Justin's voice behind me is tinged with laughter.

"I…" *I don't know what you'll expect from me if you give me a ride home.*

"You *are*…" He's still smiling. That's good. "Have you still not figured out how irresistible I am?"

"What?" Is he serious?

"I'm kidding, Joy." He shakes his head.

"It's just…"

"All I want is to talk with you outside of class. Just a ride. I'll drop you off, and that's it." He holds his hands out, palms up. "Promise."

"That's it?" I'm leaning toward him I want to believe him so bad; there's just this other side of me that knows we're about to be in a car together, and I'm not sure that's a good idea.

"Yeah. Totally not a big deal. Just a ride."

Okay. Totally no big deal. I can do this. Now I just need to say something. "Where's your car?"

"Come on." He gestures toward the school lot with his head.

We walk together through the downpour to a sad, faded black car.

"So, this is it." He opens the passenger door for me.

"Cool." That feels like the right thing to say.

He chuckles. "Not so much, no. But it's what I could afford." He closes the door behind me and gets in on his side.

I take in a deep breath. Okay, I'm okay. I'm in a car, alone with a boy. I try to take another breath and it's shaky. "I need my window down."

He pauses. "It's cold outside. And raining."

"Please?" I'd rather ask him for something crazy than hyperventilate.

The small car rattles as the engine warms up and I roll my window down. As insane as having the window down seems, or, I guess, as insane as it *is*, I have an escape so I feel okay in here. I'm *so* not putting *needs an open window* on my list of crazy things. I'm in the car. That counts for something.

"You're really quiet."

"You're just now noticing?" Listen to me, teasing him and everything. I definitely need to call Lydia.

"No. We've been in school for two months, and it took me that long to ask you out, and then you sort of said no." We're in a line of cars waiting to get out of the school parking lot.

"I said maybe," I correct him.

"Why didn't you say yes?" he asks as he gives me a glance.

"I...I don't know." Mostly because I'm still scared.

"It's cool we're talking though."

"What?"

"I've just... I've wanted to talk since you came to school, but... I guess I'm a coward or something." He smiles.

I'm not sure what to make of him yet. "Oh."

The line inches forward, and Justin flips on the radio, tapping his steering wheel to the beat. I watch, envious at how relaxed he seems.

We finally pull out of the lot and onto the roadway.

"Wanna get a hot chocolate or a coffee or something on the way back?"

"Drive-through?" I ask. "Or..."

"Whichever."

"Drive-through."

"You got it."

And I'm okay in here, because this is the only situation I have to worry about dealing with. Just me, in his car. Even crazy Joy can drink out of a cup in front of Justin.

Maybe I do have a chance at normal. Wouldn't that be something?

ELEVEN
AN OUTING

I let out a sigh as we pull up my driveway. Three extra cars are parked in front of the house. My stomach sinks. "My cousin's home. With friends."

"Right, the mighty Trent Mooreson." Justin puts his car in park, turns it off, but doesn't move.

"He's not mighty anything. He's probably the only one here that I just don't get." I take another sip of hot chocolate. I'm not in a hurry to get out of the car, not with Trent and his gang inside.

"You live with your aunt and uncle, right?" Justin asks. He pulls a knee up and leans back.

My heart's hammering. This is how the hard to answer questions start. "Yeah." I don't want to lie to him again—then I'll just have to *tell* him I lied again—sometime later, when I get the guts to.

"And that's better than home?" His eyes are on me.

My eyes are on my cup. "Home doesn't exist anymore." I take

another drink, which is only a temporary distraction from my thoughts.

"I'm guessing that answer is code for you're done talking about this." His voice is still so relaxed.

"Yeah." The word comes out in a breath of relief.

"Okay." He tilts his head way back and takes the last drink of his coffee, holding the cup up and tapping the bottom to make sure he gets every drop.

"You're funny." I'm watching him. He's not much bigger than me—lean and only slightly taller. Much less intimidating than… almost every guy I've had contact with.

"Glad you think so. I'm just trying to get my money's worth of caffeine." He chuckles again as he puts his cup into the cup holder.

I like his talking, the way he moves. I like watching him.

Uncle Rob's silver SUV pulls in next to us. "There's my uncle. I should go." Probably best in case he starts asking questions I'm not sure how to answer.

"Let me get your door, okay? Make me feel like I actually took you out, even though I just drove you home." He jumps out and runs around the front of his car.

"Okay." I sit and wait and it seems sort of silly. But he opens my door and offers his hand to help me out.

I can't take it. Touch feels like a whole different level of closeness, and I just can't.

And I thought I was doing so well.

His hand hanging in the air is like a reminder that I may have let him drive me home, but I'm still pathetic.

Uncle Rob saves me. "Hey, Joy."

Justin reaches his hand out to shake Uncle Rob's. "I'm Justin, a friend of Joy's from government class."

I jump out before he can offer me his hand again.

Uncle Rob looks between us a few times as I get out.

"Did Trent forget you?" Uncle Rob asks.

"No." I shake my head. "Justin offered me a ride, which turned out better anyway because Trent has a bunch of friends over." I glance again at the extra cars in the driveway.

"Okay. Well, thank you, Justin." Uncle Rob's eyes go back to him. "You're Tom's son, right?"

"Yeah," Justin answers.

I'm standing next to him now and he smiles at me again. His smile sends these happy warm tingles all through me. It's kind of strange to have a boy like him like me. He has to like me, right? Isn't that what feeling this excitement is all about?

"I'll see you at school tomorrow." He waves and climbs back into his car.

"He seems nice," Uncle Rob says as he watches me.

"He is." My eyes focus on the front door, which feels much safer than looking at Uncle Rob.

"Ready to head in?" he asks.

I shake my head. Holding myself together for that long car ride with Justin wore me out. Trent's friends are sure to put me over the edge.

"You don't have to, Joy, but do you want to go somewhere with me?"

"Where?" It comes out before I have a chance to filter it. The destination really shouldn't matter.

"Just a few minutes down the road. I thought we'd get you a phone." He's standing patiently, even though the rain is really coming down.

"For what?"

He chuckles. "So friends, like Justin, can call you. So when you decide to get a ride home with someone we've never met, you can tell us first. When you decide you want to run to the mall on your own like Tara does nearly every afternoon, you can call home if you need a ride. Or we can call you if we're worried. It was one thing when you were with Tara or Trent all the time, but now you're doing things on your own, and I want you to have that freedom but also the safety in knowing you can reach us. So, you know, normal stuff."

"None of that seems normal." Though I don't really know what normal is. "I'm sorry. I didn't really think about if it was okay for Justin to give me a ride."

"It's okay." He nods. "My guess is that you'd be a lot more careful than most."

I don't say anything, but I have to agree.

"Anyway, I know his dad. Good man." He takes a step back toward his car. "Wanna head out?"

"Okay." I jog around the front of the SUV because I don't want him to have to wait for me and climb in. Now I'm in Uncle Rob's car. Just a month ago I couldn't bring myself to talk to him.

"Ready?" His voice is loud as he climbs in on his side.

I jump and lean toward the door. Totally involuntary. Totally makes me a coward.

"I'm sorry, Joy. I forget." He sits still for a moment, his voice barely above a whisper. "We don't have to do this."

"I'm just tired." I rub my forehead with my hand. "I talked with Justin all the way home from school and we stopped for hot chocolate, and..." It's nothing that should leave me feeling so wiped out.

"And that kind of energy is exhausting. I get it." His smooth voice is back. "Tell you what. We get there, and you change your mind about any part of this or want to sit in the car while I go inside, you just let me know, okay?"

"Thanks." I let my head rest back and close my eyes.

Uncle Rob doesn't talk and I don't talk during the drive. I think about my short time with Justin this afternoon. I'm sort of in shock that I rode with him. I may be nervous around him, but I'm not afraid to talk to him anymore. That feels big. Significant.

"We're here." Uncle Rob turns the car off. "Do you want to come in?"

I open my eyes to a small storefront that looks nearly empty inside. I should be able to do this. Nothing bad has ever happened to me in a *cell phone* store. I'm good.

I grab the door handle and step out.

"Okay." Uncle Rob jumps out his side and we walk in together.

I'm overwhelmed by the choices. There must be more than a hundred kinds of phones here.

"Do you know what you want?" Uncle Rob asks.

He stands close, but it feels more like protection than anything else, which helps me relax. Even two weeks ago the idea that Uncle Rob close to me could be relaxing would have felt impossible. It's proof that I can do better—move forward. All of those things that Lydia spouts at me.

"I want something really, really simple." None of the phones look like phones, they're all like small computers.

"Let's just go the counter, then."

"Okay." I follow. Having my own phone—just the idea of it makes me feel grown-up. Independent.

He talks with the cashier in a language I barely understand. I look at the large TVs on the walls, advertising phones and apps and plans. It seems kind of silly since we're in the store with the actual products all around.

"Here." Uncle Rob hands me a phone. "It'll take us a few more minutes to get it set up."

The phone's front slides open for me to take calls. I feel myself smile. I slide it up and then back down. Cool.

The door is shoved open by a couple of guys, probably Uncle Rob's age, but not as neat. I turn away and lean against the counter next to my uncle. He'll be like my wall so they're not really there.

One of the two men stands in line behind us. I breathe in and smell Marlboro smoke. That smell is so connected to Mom's trailer.

To the men there. To the glances, which led to touches which led to…My lungs seize up. I choke. I need to get out. Now.

I tug Uncle Rob's sleeve. "Uncle Rob?" I whisper.

He's digging through his wallet. "Yeah?"

"I need to go—now."

He doesn't hesitate. "I'll be back in a moment," he says to the cashier as we move for the door. I take a deep breath as we step outside. The clean air immediately helps, but I'm still shivering.

"I'm sorry, Joy. I wasn't paying attention." He's looking at me with the same sympathetic frown as when he saw my scars.

He stops next to the passenger door of his SUV. "Are you okay?"

The words bounce around inside me, bringing tears to the surface. "I'm so tired of being afraid of nothing." I fold my arms. The pavement feels like the only safe place to look.

"It's not nothing." He shakes his head. "Climb in. Relax on your own. I'll be back with your phone."

I want to throw up. I'm so pathetic there aren't words to describe me in this moment. A smell and a loud voice and suddenly I can't function. I hate being such a mess. I jerk open the car door and slip inside.

I focus on Uncle Rob in the store. The two guys are still standing behind him in line. Something about how they move and shove each other reminds me of some of Mom's friends. I can almost feel the unwanted hands on me and I squirm in my seat, wishing that closing my eyes would help push the memory away. That life is back in California. I tell myself this over and over.

A world away. A lifetime away. I'm not there anymore.

I know this part. The part I can't believe is that I might never have to be there again.

"Here you go."

I jump, not realizing Uncle Rob's returned.

He hands me my phone. "You're one number off the whole rest of the family."

"I'm sorry you had to—"

"Joy." His smile is wide. "You're out with me. That alone is kind of a big deal for me. As a dad, I have this insane desire to protect you, to protect Trent—who wants no part of my protection—and to protect Tara."

I don't fully understand, so I sit silent, hoping he'll continue.

"Joy, if you didn't think I was crazy, I'd sit next to you all the time, and drive you places you want to go, because I want to make sure you're safe. And not just that you're physically safe, but that you *feel* safe too. It's a dad thing." He puts the car in gear and pulls out.

"I feel safe with you," I say.

"Good." He smiles. "You have no idea how happy that makes me. Maybe this is the first of many outings." He lets out a long breath. "Think about what you want for dinner, and we'll pick it up on the way home."

"Anything?" I ask, my mind spinning with possibilities. Have I ever picked out dinner before? So many choices and possibilities and people to please…

"Anything."

Before letting myself overthink, I say, "Pizza."

"Perfect." He smiles wide, and I guess that's it. We're getting pizza tonight because it's what *I* want. Amazing.

It's still the simple things in my new life that overwhelm me.

TWELVE
CONTROL

A week's gone by and I have yet to use my new phone. Maybe it's good that I haven't needed anything. Aunt Nicole hands me another dish, which I set in the dishwasher.

Trent sits by the front door in Nike shorts and a white T-shirt attacking his phone with his thumbs. This is what he does with most of his Saturdays unless he's out with friends.

"Rob!" Aunt Nicole calls. "You two are going to be late!"

"He can wait!" Uncle Rob laughs from upstairs.

"What are they doing?" I ask as I add detergent and start the full machine. This has been my chore for the past week, and it's such an easy one that I'm happy to feel like I'm helping.

"Trent and Uncle Rob do kung fu together. They have for ages. Trent's busier than he used to be, but they still like the workout."

Uncle Rob steps into the kitchen and kisses Aunt Nicole on the cheek.

"Can I come?" The words fly out of my mouth before I have a

chance to stop them.

Uncle Rob's brows go up. "Yeah. Why don't you change into those soft pants your mom got you, that way if you feel like joining, you can."

Aunt Nicole's face pulls into wrinkles of worry. "It's loud, Joy, and…"

I've already decided and want to go before I think too much and chicken out. "I'll be right back." I jog upstairs, take off my button-up from school, and throw on a T-shirt and the yoga pants from my aunt.

Wait. Uncle Rob called Aunt Nicole my mom. My heart aches for it. I know the word slip was just a stupid mistake on his part so why does it have to give me so much hope?

I almost run into Tara at the top of the stairs.

"Where are you off to?" she asks.

"Kung fu?" I didn't think when I first asked. My note to Lydia's going to be a good one.

Tara makes a face. "Have fun with that."

"I'm curious." I shrug and run downstairs.

"Ready?" Uncle Rob's smile is wide, but his voice is soft and quiet, like it always is around me.

"Yeah." I'm brave. I'm strong. I'm so going to do something I've never done.

Now I can be Joy, Queen of New Experiences.

There are more people at the kung fu studio than I was expecting.

Mirrors run along one side and mats lay on the floor. The group is diverse, with some women—maybe two or three—a lot of men, and a few kids my age.

Uncle Rob stops next to me as Trent moves on to the massive mat. "The instructor's loud. Don't let it bother you. It's just what he does, okay?"

I nod.

"You want to leave, just make eye contact with me or run out to the car."

"All right." I have a way out, which makes the whole new experience fun instead of panic-inducing.

I sit on the floor near the door to watch because I'm not sure what to expect. Everyone says their hellos and spreads out on the mats, starting with lunges. The instructor is strong and flexible, stretching farther than anyone else and looks like he's straining *less* than everyone else. A girl with long pigtails and bleach blond hair is in the back corner close to where I'm sitting, and I watch her.

Her jaw flexes as she stretches, almost as close to the mat as the instructor. Her eyes seem focused directly in front of her, not even really watching the teacher. She looks so...*tough*.

Her eyes catch mine, and she smiles big. She has a ring. *In her lip.* I cringe. That had to hurt. We're about the same height, but that's where the similarities end. She has gorgeous almond-shaped eyes and darker skin, an odd contrast to her bleached hair. Her body is straight and strong. She stands in a way that puts me in awe of her.

"Come on." She jerks her head for me to join her.

I shake my head. Watching is enough for today.

"Come on." She jerks her head again.

I fold my arms.

She walks over. "You can't let the boys have all the fun. Just try it." She reaches out a hand, and my hand reaches out to take it. I have no idea how that happened. She lifts me to my feet.

"I'm Daisy."

"Joy."

"Cool." She grins. "You can hang with me."

We step onto the mat, and no one even glances my way. I'm just one of many.

"Horse!" the instructor yells from the front.

"Like this." She widens her stance and crouches low.

I do the same.

"Good. Now hold it for as long as you can. He's brutal and will make us all sit like this until people start to collapse."

She giggles and I feel my mouth pull into a smile.

My legs start to burn. Like fire. But I can do pain. I've certainly felt worse.

"You can make your body do anything." The instructor's voice is so strong, so convincing. "Mind over matter, right?"

A few people chuckle.

I can do this. I can make my body do this. My legs burn, but I have control over them. I get to tell them when they can stop burning.

I focus on being still. My body relaxes into the position and even though I hurt, I feel like I could sit here indefinitely.

"We have two tough little girls in the back tonight, making you boys look like a big bunch of sissies." The instructor chuckles.

My eyes focus, and Daisy's laughing next to me. "Oh my gosh,

I'm done!" She stands and shakes her legs out.

I follow her lead, but my legs don't work right anymore, and I laugh. I rub my palms up and down the top of my rubbery thighs. That helps, but my legs still don't feel like my legs.

Uncle Rob has shifted closer to me. He gives me a thumbs-up, and a surge of pride rushes though me. Just like that, I'm hooked.

"So." Daisy puts her hands on her hips after class. "You're coming back, right?"

"I'm coming back." My whole body is loose and shaky, but I feel tough, in control, and that's something I've never felt before. I push the hair off my hot, sweaty face.

"Cool. I'm always here. My dad owns this place."

"Okay." I cross my arms but more out of habit than for protection.

"I'll see you around." She slaps my upper arm before turning toward the office.

"See you."

Uncle Rob gives me a light squeeze before holding open the door. We've never even touched before, and I didn't even flinch. Definite progress.

"You did good," he says as we step outside.

Trent's laughing with a guy taller than him who follows us out.

"Good one, Mooreson." The guy's startling blue eyes catch mine. "Nice job in there," he says to me.

I don't speak. I don't know him.

"See you later." He laughs loudly, slaps Trent on the back, and jogs off to his car.

Trent laughs. "Well, don't tell Tara that Brandon spoke to you. She's had a crush on him since freshman year." Trent rolls his eyes like he doesn't think she's good enough for Brandon, which is ridiculous.

"I didn't know that," Uncle Rob says slowly. He turns and frowns as the Brandon kid pulls out of the lot.

"And watch out for Daisy," Trent says to me. "She's an awesome girl, but she'll do *anything*." Trent chuckles and then adds more quietly, "Daisy parties are legendary. If you're invited, always say yes."

"Let's go," Uncle Rob says as he waits at the driver's side door.

Trent glances at me. "You got the front seat on the ride over. You can take the back on the ride home."

That seems fair enough. It's what he'd do with Tara anyway. I pull open the back door.

"Trent," Rob warns.

"It's fair," I say as I climb in the back before Uncle Rob can say anything else and before Trent has more cause to be annoyed with me.

I close my eyes in the backseat and wonder when I'll be able to go back to Kung Fu.

When we get home, I pull out my notebook and write,

° *Joy does kung fu.*

I'm still high from my night and feel amazing.

THIRTEEN
FORGOTTEN THINGS

Justin's standing at the end of the driveway when I step outside Monday morning. This is the first time I've seen him outside of school since he gave me a ride home, and my heart does a little jump.

"Morning," Justin says with a smile I can barely see under the hood of his raincoat. "Are you waiting for me?" I ask as I adjust my hood under the falling rain. I'm feeling this confidence I've ever felt before. My legs still burn with every step after kung fu on Saturday, but the soreness is all from me. In my control. School should be *easy* today.

"Maybe a little." Justin does this really cute thing where he tries to hold in his smile but half fails.

Today I keep my eyes on him long enough to appreciate the dimple in his cheek. "Okay."

"You seem happy today," he says as we start up the street together.

"Have you ever done kung fu?"

"Used to a bit." He walks a couple sideways steps to look at me around his hood. "I'm guessing you have?"

"Yeah. Saturday night. It was fun."

"Your first time?"

I nod and keep my eyes on him as we walk. If I can beat some of the men in horse stance, I can certainly look at Justin.

"How are your legs?"

"Super rubbery." I laugh a little.

He nods like he understands.

Everything about our simple chats still feel like a big deal to me, and I'm starting to settle into the idea that simple things *will* feel like big things for a while.

"You going again?" he asks.

"Definitely."

"Good. Not enough girls do kung fu. Gotta even out the playing field a little." He gestures in front of him. "Did you meet a Daisy?"

"A Daisy?"

"Crazy half-Asian girl? Tougher than nails? A little loud?" He laughs.

"How do you know her?"

Justin snorts. "Everyone knows Daisy. She's homeschooled but there's not a party that Daisy doesn't find her way into if she wants to be there. Also she's amazing at kung fu and won some national stuff with that, so she's a bit of a celebrity in our small suburb of Seattle..."

"You're friends?" I ask, wanting to know more. Maybe a few people I know could know each other. I think about how Trent invites people over. How Tara has girls she eats lunch with. Maybe I'll get to have my own group.

"Oh yeah. Her family's kung fu studio has been in this neighborhood for years. I think everyone has gone to their family nights at least a few times."

"Oh." Kind of like how people in the trailer park all sort of knew each other. Well, sort of knew each other. "Where's your car?" I ask.

He sighs but with a wide smile. "So, the thing about old, cheap, crappy cars is they don't always run…"

"Bummer."

He lightly bumps his arm against mine. "I'm walking with you, so it all worked out."

I have to look away because my cheeks heat up so fast there's no way he won't notice. But I'm not scared. I'm flattered. That feels like a million steps in a good direction.

I look around the school as I head to first period. Something obvious strikes me as I stand in the middle of the commons area. I'm maybe one of them. I mean, I know I've come to school for about two months, but now I think I might belong here. In a school with kids my age. Kids who will go to college and do big things and live good lives. The feeling is both overwhelming and amazing, even though I should have felt this way from day one.

I grasp the railing to help my sore legs up the stairs and pause at the top when I see a huge bulletin board of sketches. I step closer and take in the pencil strokes and shading, seeing how people did it perfectly, and wishing I could smudge or erase bits on others. Another realization pushes into me. I miss drawing enough to try it out again.

The bell rings and my heart leaps up my throat. Crap! I'm *never* late. I forget for a moment which class I'm supposed to be in, and the second it hits me, I spin around and smash into someone, scattering my books, notebook, and pens across the floor.

"Dammit!" A guy yells.

I drop to my knees and stop, one hand on my books and the other on my chest where my heart is sprinting.

"Watch where you're going!"

I stay frozen on the floor until his footsteps fade. I'm so stupid. I need to be more careful. I gather my stuff with trembling fingers, and, pulling in a slow breath, I try to slow my heart

When lunch comes, I hide to make sure I'm out of the way. I keep my eyes down and leave the school the second the final bell rings to avoid walking home with Justin or Tara. I'm just too tired for people today. Sucks how quickly I'm back to feeling so small.

FOURTEEN
IS THIS WHAT WE CALL A BREAKTHROUGH?

I'm standing in Lydia's very beige waiting room with Uncle Rob. We both stare at the fish tank in silence because there's really nothing else to look at, and after a few minutes of questions in the car, I think he gave up trying to talk to me.

My day, which started with Justin and talking and sore legs and pride, ended with me hiding even more than I did two weeks ago. Only now I know how good it feels to take in my surroundings. I talked to Justin and watched people interact in the hallways instead of staring my shoes. Now I want to disappear. The familiar weight in my chest is something I thought I'd gotten rid of.

Lydia steps out of her office. Her eyes go from Uncle Rob to me. "Oh, good. Uncle Rob can come in with us today."

Of course she'd do this to me. Uncle Rob was proud of me last night, but what will happen when he sits in and realizes I slid right back to where I was before? He'll probably think kung fu was a waste.

"So you two are talking," Lydia says. She crosses her legs and rests her notebook on her lap.

"He let me come to kung fu," I say quietly because that's the only thing I want to talk about today.

"How was that?" she asks, a tinge of uncertainty in her voice.

"She did amazing." Uncle Rob's eyes catch Lydia's first and then mine.

My chest swells at the compliment.

We talk about inconsequential things for a few minutes. Most of our back and forth has to do with Uncle Rob saying how different I am, how much more relaxed I seem in the house.

His observations cut both ways for me. Part of me is proud I've come so far and part of me hates that we have to be here having this conversation. Walking around in a house shouldn't be praiseworthy.

"Do you have anything to say?" Lydia focuses on me.

The clock ticks. No one speaks. I used to take pride in the silence I created with Lydia, but now it seems like…It seems pointless.

"I used to be afraid of him. Of Uncle Rob, but…"

"Why don't you tell him?" Lydia asks.

Right. Uncle Rob and I are good now. This is okay. I angle my body to see him better. "I'm sorry I was afraid of you."

"No, Joy…" he starts.

"Let her finish." Lydia's voice is quiet.

I need to get this out. I'm desperate for Uncle Rob to still be proud of me. For him to know I think he's nice. "I wasn't afraid of *you*, not really. It's like…like my body's trying to protect me, so when you'd talk or were around me, my body wanted to get away, even though logically, I knew you wouldn't hurt me. At least I did after a while." I wonder if I'm making any sense because it feels like I had to push out every word, and I'm not sure I could do it again.

Uncle Rob shifts in his seat, but his eyes remain on me. "You're a very brave girl."

I laugh, but it's not really a laugh. It's hard and forced. "I'm not brave. It took me four months to talk to you. I'm still afraid of everything, all the time. I felt so strong this morning, and then when I went to school…I had a hard time. I hide in my room, I…" The list is so long.

"I still think you're very brave."

My eyes go to my lap. "Thanks," I mumble. Uncle Rob being proud of me feels impossible because of what I mess I am, so his words don't feel genuine.

"How are we doing with family meals and that kind of thing?" Lydia asks.

I shrug.

"Better," he says.

"Joy, maybe this week…just keep going what you're doing, okay? Spend time with your new family." Her eyes are on me. "And *you* forgot to waste time today. Our time's up."

Already? Time here usually drags.

"Let's meet once a week. See how you do with that. And you know you can call anytime. Okay?"

"Once a week?" That feels way less like I'm an insane person than coming in twice a week.

"Maybe you could do kung fu on the other night, huh?"

"Yes." Uncle Rob stands. "We can definitely do that."

And that's it. Maybe my afternoon was just a little slip. Maybe I can keep doing better.

"How can you be sixteen and never played Yahtzee?" Trent's eyes are wide, and there's even a hint of annoyance in his voice.

"My mom had cards. I've never played anything but cards."

The Mooresons still seem pretty unusual to me. A couple times a month, they all sit together and play board games or card games. Tonight's the first night I'm joining in. It's part of my assignment from Lydia, and one I'm determined to do.

"That's insane." Trent leans over the table toward me.

I shrug.

"Trent." Uncle Rob gives him a stern look.

I notice all these little things now because I'm not staring at my lap with the family anymore.

"Here's a breakdown of how the scores work." Aunt Nicole slides the sheet over to me.

I read the rules while Trent writes names on the scorecard because apparently he doesn't trust us to be honest or add correctly. I don't really trust *him*, but I'm not going to argue when we're getting along.

After an hour, I'm only a few points behind Trent, but he still wins in the end. I'm okay with that. I now know how to play a game. And I survived sitting with the whole family.

Tara stands. She hugs her mom and then her dad, just like every night. Trent does the same, only he's too cool for a real hug. He does a half hug. He doesn't know what it's like to have a parent who doesn't hug.

"Thanks." I put my arms cautiously around Aunt Nicole first.

Uncle Rob gives me a smile and a nod like every night. Even on the nights I don't look directly at him. But Uncle Rob isn't scary anymore. I watch my feet as I step toward him. Does he want me to hug him? Does he want to hug me? "Thanks, that was fun."

"I'm really glad you joined us." His voice is soft and warm. He's a dad. It's all he wants. He's not going to try for more than that, he's not going to ask for more than that, and he definitely won't force more than that.

My heart's beating hard, but I lean into him anyway. I wrap my arms around him and squeeze. My face is pressed into his chest. I never thought it would feel good to be close to a man like this. Ever. But his chest is warm and comforting, not suffocating.

His arms are careful but relaxed around me. "I love you, Joy." He kisses the top of my head. Part of me never wants to move. But that's just weird, isn't it? To just stand with someone like that.

"Night." I drop my arms and walk away. I glance back quickly. Just long enough to see him wiping tears from his face again.

For as hard as I worked to make my mom love me, I wonder a

lot if she ever did. I've done nothing here but cause disruption, but I'm told I'm loved. I'm once again overwhelmed by the feeling in this house.

FIFTEEN
SOME THINGS HURT WORSE THAN OTHERS

Aunt Nicole stands in the kitchen with an envelope in her hands. "I feel weird about giving this to you, but I also feel weird not giving it to you."

"What is it?"

"One of the cases was resolved without a trial." Her voice is low, quiet. She's looking at me with so much worry. I'm still baffled by the idea of her feeling so much for me.

Shaking, I stare at the envelope, afraid to touch the letter. "Oh." Only two people are in jail because of me. I was asked for names of others, but I didn't want to relive anything that far in my past, so I never said. "Mom?"

She shakes her head.

Richard. The force of his name leaves me exhausted. His face hits my memory and I have to push it away. Hard. I can't go there. I stumble back and lean against the wall. Better. Safer.

Only I'm staring at what's just paper. All the actions they've wrapped up in the notifications inside that envelope are gone. Done. Over.

I wonder if I was supposed to be notified before the case was resolved. I wonder if Uncle Rob and Aunt Nicole knew but were just protecting me.

"The DA faxed this over, and we spoke on the phone earlier today. The defendant will be in jail for fifteen years." Aunt Nicole's voice is quiet, but her words split into me as if she'd screamed them.

Fifteen years for what he did to me. That's it. But in a way it doesn't even matter. I'm gone from there. I'm here. In other ways the sentence or lack thereof is sort of everything. How can being stuck in a prison for fifteen years make up for anything? What does it change? He can't take his actions back. And he probably wouldn't if he could.

I take the envelope from Aunt Nicole and walk into Uncle Rob's den. I flip the switch for the fire and sit, no longer able to keep Richard's face away. His mouth against mine, always stubbly, leaving red marks on my skin. The smell of beer and cigarette smoke hits my nose as if he's standing in the room. I swallow down bile as my stomach tightens. He was so big, so tall and broad, and I tried to fight, I tried so hard. But my hands were tiny, and he just laughed. Then he started bringing a knife. It only made things worse, trying to fight him. When he pushed back it hurt. Richard always found creative ways to punish me.

Aunt Nicole's next to me, her arm around me. The paper is crumpled in my fist. I have no idea when either of these happened, but I'm grateful for both. I bury my face in her shoulder and let the sobs shake my body.

"You're growing up so pretty, Joy." His voice is gruff and sends a wave of chills through me. He stands in the doorway of my room. The dim light almost makes the situation worse. His face is shaped in shadows, not light.

I hate Richard.

My breathing is coming in tight, shallow breaths. What does he want? Richard has stared at me in ways that make me hide in my room, but he's never come in here.

"Mom?" My voice wobbles.

He chuckles. "Your mom is out for the night, leaving me a little wanting."

Wanting what? I pull my blankets more tightly around me as he steps into my room. Do I scream? Do I run? Do I need to?

When his heavy body crushes my thin mattress to the floor I begin to shake.

"Relax, Joy." His gravelly voice brings a whimper up my throat.

His hand is over my mouth so hard my jaw aches and my head is pressed into my pillow. I squeeze my eyes tight. I don't know what he wants, but I hope it doesn't last long.

His cigarette breath and beer stench hit my nose as his scratchy face presses against mine. "Make a noise, and I'll kill you."

I nod so he knows I believe him. My breath comes hard and fast out my nose, his hand still firmly over my mouth.

He slides off my shirt, and I close my eyes wishing to be anywhere else. I whimper as a small slice of pain flashes across my chest. I open my eyes to see a small knife. "I'll use this. Deeper next time if I have to. Remember to be good."

I shut my eyes, wishing it to be over.

His hand comes off my mouth and I want to scream so badly, but I know how to stay silent. I've been practicing for years.

I sit up in bed and scream. It feels so good to let it out. How many times had I clenched my teeth together to stop from making a sound? My heart beats hard, my breath comes fast, just as if I were there. Just like it wasn't another nightmare.

Aunt Nicole flies into my room. I ache to be wrapped up in her arms, but I can't say what I want. Can't ask her to do anything else for me.

"I'll flip my own pillow." I keep my eyes away from hers, roll my pillow over, and lie back down. I don't smell my sheets. I smell the trailer, beer, and cheap aftershave.

I'm here. I'm not there. I'm here. I'm not there.

"Night," she whispers.

My first tears hit the pillow as she leaves the room.

SIXTEEN

I HAVE DECIDED I NOW LOVE THE PARK

I'm at the park near our house, and I'm alone, sitting crisscross applesauce on the grass. I love it. If I need something or feel a panic attack coming on or anything, I have my phone. It makes me feel so much more independent than I ever have. And the open space isn't as uncomfortable as it used to be either, which is sort of perfect because I haven't seen the sun in over a month.

After several nights of horrible dreams and very little sleep, the park and the warmth should help settle my mind.

Flashes of Richard have been haunting me since the letter, making me wish again that I could erase memories. I pull in a deep breath wanting to soak up the warm day instead of reliving my past.

"Hey, neighbor."

Justin. I can so do this. I mean, we rode in a car together and talked over coffee and hot chocolate and we walk together... *sometimes.* "Hey, neighbor," I say back. Maybe he'll distract me from things I don't want to think about.

"Is the grass wet?"

"Yep, but my coat is long." I pat my hands on my hips to show the coat covers pretty well. It's Aunt Nicole's raincoat, so it's a little big, but at least I'm warm and dry.

"Oh well." He shrugs and pats his thighs. His coat is not long. "Can I sit?"

I tap my chin as if trying to decide.

"Oh, come *on*." He laughs.

"Yes, you can sit." I'm smiling and I didn't even have to think about smiling. It's like when Justin's around, there isn't room for thoughts outside of what we're doing together.

"Thank you." He's next to me, almost too close, but there are no walls out here, and I can stand up and walk away if I want to.

"You have a blond stripe in your hair," I say. Someone did the bleaching low, so the stripe only shows sometimes.

"Always had it."

I narrow my eyes. "It looks bleached."

"I swear it's always been there. The longer my hair is, the more you can see the blond." He bends his head down so I can look more closely.

"I like your hair long." Without thinking I touch the lighter strands. I wouldn't cut it any other way.

"Thanks." His eyes meet mine.

I jerk my hand back. I can't believe I just touched his hair like that.

"So, what are you up to?" he asks.

"Enjoying the sun."

"Me too."

"I got a phone." I slide it out of my pocket to show him. "Like more than a week ago. I keep forgetting I have it."

"Cool, give me your number and I can call you sometime. Or send you a text or something." He pulls out his cell.

Oh no. "I don't remember my number." How do I not know this?

"Can I see?" He reaches his hand toward me and I give the phone to him.

He pushes a few buttons on my phone and then a few buttons on his phone. "There. You can scroll down and hit the Call button when you get to my name. Have you never had a phone before?"

I try to play cool. "Why do you ask?"

"Because you're looking at this thing like it'll bite you." He chuckles as he shoves his phone back into his jeans pocket. I like how he dresses outside of school. Snug jeans, drawn-on shoes, white T-shirt, and hoodie coat. Everything looks soft. I'm probably staring.

Oh. We were talking. "I've never had a phone. I"—partial truth, I can do it—"I didn't get out much when I lived with my mom. Now I'm with my aunt and uncle and…" What do I say?

"And things are different," he finishes for me.

"Yeah." *Like opposite.* I wait for him to ask more about my mom, but he doesn't.

"So, my sister is about to have a baby and she likes to sing. I play for her when she does. Anyway, we're at the Hole next Friday night. You should come."

The Hole is a bakery and venue for a lot of great local music. *And* it's just up the street. I'm conflicted because going could be cool or disastrous. I'm not sure if it would be worth the risk.

"What do you play?"

"The guitar." He cocks a brow, throwing me a playful smile. "I thought everyone knew that."

"I didn't." I don't know anybody, so I don't know anything about anybody.

"That's crazy." He laughs. "That's like my power play, you know. The thing girls like about me."

I almost laugh. "I didn't know. So I guess that's not what I like about you."

"Hmm." His eyes are so intense, but I can't bring myself to look away. "So, what do you like about me?"

That's easy. "That you let me be quiet. I like the way you talk all relaxed and how you don't mind the weird things I do." Once the words are out I realize how personal it might all be. "I'm sorry, I..." *I don't know how to talk to people. I don't know what I should say and when I should keep quiet.* Maybe I've just crossed a line or something.

"No. That's awesome. I don't think you do weird things. I like that you're not afraid to ask to have your window down even when it's raining outside." His eyes widen, but he's smiling really big so I know he's teasing.

The teasing makes my weirdness feel okay. But now we're both quiet and the silence stretches and I don't know what to say or what he might expect from me. How long has it been? Should I say something?

Is it my turn and I messed up? "I should head back home."

"Was that silence awkward for you?" Justin asks. "'Cause I don't mind. I mean, I don't mind just hanging out with someone, even if we're quiet." He doesn't move.

"Okay."

Justin doesn't mind the quiet, which takes away all the tension that comes with trying to find the right things to say. I lean back on my hands and let my eyes drift around the park. There are families and people with dogs and couples and joggers. So many people out enjoying the unseasonably warm weather. I look up at the blue sky and the small wisps of clouds. California was always too hot. Our trailer was never cool enough. My eyes slide closed and the sun warms my face, my neck…

"You're very pretty."

I jerk my head up, fear prickling my thoughts and then down my spine, making me shiver. Why does that make me uncomfortable?

"Sorry," Justin says. "I didn't mean to interrupt you. I said I don't mind silence, and then I just spoke when I should have kept my mouth shut. But you are…pretty. Your shiny hair and pale freckles."

His words and tone and closeness suddenly are too much. Way too much. Being called pretty rakes feelings up my spine and leaves me with memories of experiences that I never want to know again.

"I should go." I stand. My breathing is still okay, but I'm noticing it now, the simple act of taking a breath. That means it's not coming normally.

"I made you uncomfortable again, huh? 'Cause I can't just shut up?" Justin's standing now too, and he's rubbing his hands on his pants. It makes him look nervous. "I'm the ADD kid, always have been. You'll get used to it." His voice is all breathless and his body looks tense. "If you don't get sick of me."

"Are you nervous?" I ask. Do other people get nervous?

He chuckles again. "Yeah. Being nervous isn't a normal thing for me. Maybe I could walk you home?"

"Okay." That seems harmless enough. And if he's nervous, I should feel safer. Like if he's more uncomfortable than me, that's a good thing.

I slide my hands into my coat pockets, and we walk through the park without saying anything. I like having him next to me. We're not touching but we're close, and I still get to people watch. There are a few skateboarders flipping their boards underneath their feet as they move. There's a couple about our age, but they can't keep their hands off each other. I look away from them. No way I could be with someone like that. I tilt my face toward the sky again. The heat from the sun is so perfect after all the rain.

"You know how I said I don't mind silence?" Justin asks.

"Yeah." I keep my gaze on the clouds.

"You totally love it, don't you?"

My eyes catch his. "I do." But I also like sharing the quiet with someone, I'm just not sure if that's something I should share.

"That's cool, but I'd still like to learn more about you, you know? Where you're from. What you like to do. You know, normal stuff." He puts his hands in his pockets.

I don't have any normal stuff. "I'm from California and just getting used to how wet it is here. Tell me about you."

"Well, it's just me and my dad. My parents got divorced a few years ago. Mom and I talk but not a lot. My big sister and her husband live not too far from here. She's going to have a baby, like, next month, so I'm about to be an uncle. Her husband owns the Hole. We used to play there even before they got together."

"Wow."

"And I like to play the guitar. No, *love* to play the guitar, but I don't want to do it as a career."

"Why not?"

"Because I'm awesome, and I don't think I'd do well with massive amounts of wealth and fame." He tries to sound so serious, but he starts laughing instead.

I laugh with him. It lightens my chest and warms me up from the inside. "You're very modest."

He laughs too. "No, I want to do graphic design. I've made like a zillion fake album covers, and I've done up Zombie IDs for all my friends."

"So you're a computer geek."

He bumps my arm with his again. "And what are you?"

"I'm…I don't know yet." That's an honest answer.

"So, really, you're Joy, the girl who's on a journey of self-discovery." I can hear the smile in his voice.

Self-discovery makes me sound so cool and way less weird. "Yeah, I guess that's me."

"So, you must be sixteen? Seventeen? I know I'm close," he teases.

"I just turned sixteen."

His brows go up. "You just *turned* sixteen?"

Why does he sound so surprised? "Yeah."

"But you're a junior."

"I tested in. Is that weird?" No one was sure where to put me, so I completed a bunch of tests when I moved here and tested into eleventh grade.

"So, you're a smart girl. That's hot." His eyes aren't on me though, not while giving me that compliment.

"You're weird." But I'm smiling, and it's the real kind.

He stops walking. "We're here."

I look up and see the house. The walk went so fast.

"I'll see you tomorrow in Government, and maybe you'll come Friday night. You can meet my sister. Daisy usually comes, so you can see her again too." He reaches out and touches just the edges of my fingers. Tingles fly up my arm and settle in my chest and then in my stomach. His fingers slide through mine, he squeezes just a little, and then backs up, letting my arm drop. He turns and walks toward his house. I'm sad to let him go, but that's about as much contact as I think I can handle right now.

As he walks away, I see the whole butt of his jeans is soaked from the grass, and I laugh. Loud.

"I know!" He laughs with me, turns, and walks backward a few steps. "But it was totally worth it."

Worth it. To sit next to me. I'm suddenly warm and tingly all over and love every second of it.

SEVENTEEN
ON THE LIST

"What is that smile about?" Tara asks as I step inside.

"It's just a nice day out today." But I know already that my red cheeks are betraying me.

She crosses her arms, disbelieving. "And that's it?"

"Justin walked me home from the park," I admit. I kick my shoes off and head into the kitchen.

"Justin *Donaldon?*" Her eyes are wide. "He used to get into a lot of trouble, but he seems a little more laid-back this year. And...he's *hot.*"

"Hey." Uncle Rob shakes his head. "Don't talk about boys like that." He's standing at the counter with a bowl of cereal in hand. "Not until you're like...thirty."

I stop and stare at Uncle Rob in old jeans and a T-shirt. "I thought you had to work today."

He shrugs. "Just this morning. I miss the construction sites because my partner is normally the one who goes out. I dropped by a couple of projects to see how things are coming along."

"But you design the houses, right? You're an...architect?" I'm interested because I miss drawing, and what Uncle Rob does can't be all that different. Homes instead of people and random objects, but still...inspired.

"I do."

"Did you design this house?" I ask as I look around the large open kitchen, wondering how much of his thought process and creativity went into this home.

"I did." He sets his bowl in the sink.

"Wow." This house feels different now, like it's more special or something because I know where it came from.

"We should take you shopping." Tara leans against the counter, crossing her arms and looking very serious.

"What?" How do we get from boys to architecture to shopping?

"You know, for clothes. I think you have school uniforms and maybe a few others things. Is that right?" she asks.

"Yeah, but I'm fine. I mean..." I'm afraid they're going to go to a lot of trouble for me. Also, school is one thing; the mall feels like a different universe.

"Dad?" Tara turns to her father, looking for help, I guess.

"I'll take you girls after I shower, okay?"

"We don't want you *there*." Tara giggles as she pulls open the fridge door.

"Just my money, is that it?" Uncle Rob teases.

The beginning twinges of panic set in. I'll be going to a mall with just Tara, without Aunt Nicole or Uncle Rob.

"I'd like you there," I say before Tara can discourage him further.

"Are you kidding?" Tara slumps, but I'm sure him coming is still okay.

"I'll stay out of the way and only speak when spoken to," Uncle Rob says. "How's that?" He winks at me.

"Fine." Tara tries to sound annoyed, but I don't think she cares either. She grabs a spoon to go with her yogurt and walks out of the room.

"Thank you." I catch Uncle Rob's eyes. "And I think it's really cool that you build houses."

"Happy to take you. And thanks for the compliment." He starts out of the kitchen. "Don't forget to eat."

I grab a banana from the counter. That'll work.

I just wish I knew what to expect from my day.

I try to pretend the mall is school. It's not working, but I have Tara and I'm desperate to be talking because it helps distract me from the chaos of the mall.

"Trent said you like Brandon," I say.

Tara's cheeks turn red. "Brandon doesn't even know I exist."

"He has to know you exist." That makes no sense. "He and Trent are friends."

She chuckles. "You don't get what I'm saying, Joy. He's not...I mean, he wouldn't go for someone like me."

"What are you talking about?" I'm confused again.

"I just...I'm not like Trent. I'm not popular like Trent."

I scramble for something to tell her to make her feel better. "Well Brandon does kung fu. Why don't you come with us?"

"'Cause I'm not good at kung fu." Now Tara's looking down like I usually do and here I am with the top of my hair pulled back off my face and walking through the mall—both are new for me.

"I still think you should come. I'd like to have you there. And maybe if you and Trent do fun stuff together, he'll be nicer with your friends and everything." I don't know if I'm helping or not. I don't know how to be around normal people, so my advice probably counts for nothing.

"Yeah, maybe I will." She bites her lip and still won't look at me. I want her to smile.

"But coming to Kung Fu should be for you, not for Brandon." I'm pretty sure doing something new shouldn't be all about the boy. Maybe there *are* benefits to being crazy enough to see a shrink.

"Well, it might be a *little* about Brandon…at first." But she's smiling and I'm thrilled because I just did something to make Tara feel better.

The dressing room is too small. I feel trapped but also exposed by the idea of actually getting naked in here. There's a stack of things that Tara found for me, but I don't think I can try them on. What will she think?

Maybe I can just choose a few items without trying them on. Then I won't have to get undressed. But I can't pick things out.

Uncle Rob will have to pay for them. The whole situation feels too weird. I have clothes. I'm fine. I don't need this. My chest gets tighter with each thought.

"I need air." I step out of my dressing room.

"Joy?" Tara calls. "I'm not dressed. *Wait*. I'll be there in a sec."

I don't wait. My legs carry me out of the dressing room to the counter.

"Can I help you?" The cashier's friendly smile doesn't feel friendly. Her disdain is probably in my head, but it doesn't change the fact that I want to get away from her and away from the tiny dressing rooms and the heap of clothes Tara found.

Where's Uncle Rob?

I start down the aisle that I think leads out of the store. Now that I don't have Tara with me, the store seems to have grown. I need to go back to her.

"Hey!" A man's voice behind me makes me jump. I look down, fold my arms, and move faster.

"I said *hey*!"

The voice is louder.

He must be gaining on me.

"You're Trent's cousin, right?" He's definitely closer.

Dread. The tingly kind that makes me see spots. He knows who I am. I need Uncle Rob.

My phone. I have a phone. I dig through my pocket and grasp it tightly.

"Hey!" The guy grabs my arm from behind.

I whimper, and my legs collapse underneath me. My heart's loud in my ears.

"Whoa." He steps back with his hands in the air, staring at where I hit the floor.

"Joy?" Uncle Rob's next to me in a moment. I don't know where he came from, and I don't care.

"I'm just looking for Trent." The guy's voice is so full of irritation, like I'm the one who just chased him down or something.

"Well, call his *phone*," Uncle Rob snaps.

I'm such an idiot. I go to school with this guy and now I feel crazy again. Why couldn't I just turn and talk to him? I suck in a breath, but my lungs aren't working right and I'm gasping for air.

"Come on." Uncle Rob helps me off the floor.

I'm afraid to look up. People staring won't help me now. Do I get to add this to my list of crazy?

○ *Can't try on clothes at the mall.*
○ *Freaks out when recognized.*

Uncle Rob digs into his pocket and hands me a small white pill—the ones set aside for panic attacks.

Defeat.

I take it.

"Here." He hands me a bottled water to wash my pill down, and my day is about to fade into nothing.

We sit in Uncle Rob's SUV and my eyes are closed. We're waiting for Tara and whatever she picks from the pile of clothes she originally chose for me.

I feel like such a wimp. "So, I'm crazy enough that you feel the need to keep drugs on your person at all times?" I ask Uncle Rob.

"It's not like that." His voice is just above a whisper. He's watching me so carefully.

"It *is* like that. I feel so weak." My body doesn't feel stressed anymore, though. I'm too relaxed and rubbery to be stressed. My thoughts are turning fuzzy like they always do on my panic meds. The tightness from my chest is gone and taking a deep breath is so *easy*. Why wasn't breathing this easy before?

"What do you mean?" he asks.

"Like you all have to be careful around me. I have this list of crazy things I do. I hate it." My list…My brain is seriously blurring out. My eyelids are so *heavy*.

"List?"

"The eating thing and the talking thing and the freak-out thing. I'm so broken." And knowing how broken I am makes me heavy, but not really sad because I can't really *feel* my brokenness right now— not after my pill.

"You have a list?"

Oops. The list was supposed to be private. I stay silent.

"Joy, you're not broken. It's…"

"I don't need one of those pills every time something goes wrong." I'm going to be a zombie for an entire day.

"I just worry, and…"

"Okay!" Tara gushes as she opens the car door. "You're going to *love* what I got you!"

"Thanks," I mumble.

The clothes and her niceness make me heavier. Poor Uncle Rob had to come to the mall, drag me out there, and pay for my stuff. Tara was stuck trying things on alone and had to make decisions for me. It's all too much. Even after the pill, I still care about what a ridiculous ordeal I turned our outing into.

EIGHTEEN
OVERHEARD

I'm pretty sure it's close to midnight, but Uncle Rob and Aunt Nicole are talking downstairs. After my pill this afternoon, I napped enough that I'm sure I won't sleep much tonight so I strain to listen.

"So the guy pled out, but her mom's still holding on?" Uncle Rob asks.

"I tried to see if I could talk to her," Aunt Nicole says. "But she won't take calls from me."

"This isn't fair. Joy shouldn't have to do anything else."

"It's not up to us. My sister is selfish. She might push the trial just because she can. She's looking at a lot of jail time for this. It's not something she's going to go quietly into." Aunt Nicole sounds apologetic.

I knew Mom would put up a fight. She never thought anything she was accused of could possibly be her fault.

Testifying for the grand jury was the worst part of all the talking I had to do about my experiences with Mom. But the prosecutor let me testify over the phone instead of in person. Lydia gave me some extra antianxiety meds and I sat on the couch and answered questions. The hearing sucked, but it felt like I was doing something that would help me later. And I guess my testimony did. I'm still with Aunt Nicole and Uncle Rob, and my mom is in jail.

"Guess she would put up a fight." Uncle Rob's voice is so quiet I barely hear him.

"I need sleep." Aunt Nicole yawns out the last half.

"I'll be up in a minute. I need more thinking time."

Their words make sense, but don't. I was warned by the prosecutor and Lydia that I might have to testify again. I'm hoping I'll have more time away from all the court stuff before I have to face the memories from my old life, but I can answer questions on the phone if the prosecutor needs me to.

I hear Aunt Nicole's bedroom door close, and I tiptoe down to see Uncle Rob on the floor in front of the fire. His legs are crossed and his elbows rest on his knees. The rest of the house is dark, quiet.

I walk slowly to the door. "Uncle Rob?" I whisper.

He jumps. "Oh, Joy. You scared me."

"Sorry, I don't want to disturb…"

"Come in." He waves me in. "If you want."

I step inside and sit close to him. Uncle Rob has turned into a safe place fast.

The fire flickers in front of us. The yellow flames have a less blue in them than normal, making the gas fire seem a little more real. Rob gives me a gentle half-squeeze. It's so different than how

I've been touched my whole life. This is for comfort, for me, nothing else.

"Why are you so sad? About me?" I ask. I'm glad I have the fire to look at.

He exhales as he drops his arm, and the room is silent. I shift a few times as I watch the patterns of flame around the pretend logs and try to ignore how long it's taking him to answer.

"I lost my sister." He sniffs. "She was…abused by some boys at school. Afterward, she was so much like you when you first got here. She wouldn't look at us. She wouldn't speak. I've stood outside your door more times than I can count just to make sure you were breathing. On the nights when I know you've had a rough day, I can't sleep. It's like you're right here so I should be able to fix everything, but I can't. There's so little I can do because you have to do so much yourself."

I sit still, waiting for him to continue.

"Each time you move forward, do something else…It gives me so much hope for you. My sister never moved forward. She retreated further and further until she took enough pills to make herself disappear."

I'm shocked into silence. Silence of breathing. Silence of thought. This is why Aunt Nicole and Uncle Rob keep my meds.

"When you have a hard day or when I see you slipping backward, I'm desperate to stop it, to make you see how amazing you are, to help you know that you have so much to look forward to. The things that happened to you won't haunt you forever."

"But I'll remember them forever." I know there's no forgetting and I'm still not sure what to do with that.

He sucks in a breath. "But they'll hurt less."

I don't have to look at him to know there are tears on his face.

"There were a few times when I didn't care if I lived or died," I tell him. "But I...I'm happy now."

He sighs. Maybe I shouldn't have said it.

"Things are going to be okay for you, Joy. You're stronger than you know." His hand rests softly on my shoulder. "I promise."

I sit on the floor with the warmth of the fire and the warmth of Uncle Rob, and I start to understand what it's like to have a dad. He cares about me. He thinks I'm strong.

I hope I won't let him down.

NINETEEN

SOMETIMES CRAPPY THINGS ARE FOLLOWED BY AWESOME THINGS AND THEN ARE FOLLOWED BY MORE CRAPPY THINGS

I'm digging around for my math book and can't find it, which means it's probably time to clean out my locker. Kind of cool that I've been at this school long enough to make a thorough mess of such a tiny space.

"Hey, you're Trent's cousin, from the mall, right?" The guy's voice is as loud as it was when he called after me the other day.

My insides immediately shake. I keep my head buried in my locker.

"What's up with you? Not gonna talk?"

I'm not going to look at him either. I squeeze my eyes tight, willing him to go away.

"What a weirdo. Joy, right?"

I open my eyes and keep digging, even though I've found what I'm looking for.

"Ty!" I hear Trent's voice from down the hall. "C'mere!"

"See ya." He leans in close to me, blowing the words into my face. I have to pull in a few deep breaths before I can turn around. Like fifteen or twenty. I stop counting at ten. The hallway is nearly empty. The bell rings, and I'm officially tardy. *Crap.* I guess this is one of those times when it's nice to be a pink-slip kid.

"You can't go to kung fu tonight!" Tara's eyes are wide. "We have to get you ready for Justin and the Hole and our night out!"

What she doesn't realize is that kung fu will help get my mind ready for tonight. Help me feel in control. Tough. I need that more than I need whatever primping she has in mind. "I'll have time. I'll just need to shower. It's just Justin, and it's just the Hole."

She rolls her eyes. "Joy, what are we going to do with you?"

"Ready?" Uncle Rob calls up.

"Come with us." I grab Tara's hand.

"Next time." She shakes her head. "I need to get ready for tonight so I can focus all my efforts on you when you come back home a big sweaty mess." She wrinkles her nose at me in mock annoyance. "But I'm glad you're having fun. My dad *can* be a cool guy."

I laugh. "Ready!" I call as I bound down the stairs to meet Uncle Rob at the front door.

"You came!" Daisy throws her arms around me. Is this normal? I barely know her.

"Your hair is pink." I stare at her as I step away.

Pink stripes run through the bleach blond.

"Not *all* of it." She looks at me like I'm crazy. Right. I'm crazy because I noticed her pink hair. I wonder how she'd look at me if she could see the list of the things that *actually* make me crazy.

"Okay," I concede. "Not all of it."

"So, let's get in there and kick some butt tonight, okay?" Her wide smile shows rows of straight white teeth.

She grabs my hand and I let her drag me into the room.

Our instructor's voice is loud, but I don't mind. He's teaching me how to be tough.

Uncle Rob and Trent take their spots. Trent's friend Brandon stands next to Trent and grins at me.

Weird.

I'm here to do kung fu, not to smile back at a guy who I don't know. This class is about me and about focusing. Nothing else.

I do all the stretches with the class to help me less sore tomorrow. Then we do some blocks and punches, always keeping our knees bent. The burn gives me power. Makes me feel in control. This is good. I can do this. I *am* doing this. In a room full of people. I'm sweaty and I'm working and I'm loving it.

Class finishes in a blink.

"You're totally hooked, aren't you?" Daisy grins.

I nod, still breathing hard and high from the exertion.

"Cool. You can come by anytime. I'm homeschooled so I'm here pretty much all day, and I get bored. Too many boys." She makes a face. "And not enough girls." She punches me in the arm.

I feel good. No, *great*. No one knows me here. All they know is that I'm the tough girl, the one who hangs with Daisy, so I get to act like I'm a tough girl. And acting like I'm stronger makes talking and being around new people so much easier.

"I'll be back," I tell her.

"You did good." Trent pats my back on the way out.

I grin until I realize Brandon's following us too.

I don't know him.

"Joy, right?" Brandon asks.

But now I'm all on edge. "Yeah." My voice is just above a whisper.

"You were awesome. I can't believe you've only come twice."

"Thanks."

I totally just said two things to a guy I don't know. "Tara's going to start coming with me," I say and wait to see if I get a reaction from him.

"See you guys later." He waves and jogs to his car.

Trent looks down at me. "Tara's not his type," he whispers, "or they'd be together by now."

"Oh." Tara's not his type? That kind of sucks. What will Tara do if the boy she likes doesn't like her?

"You coming?" Uncle Rob asks.

"Yep." Coming so I can go home and get ready to go to the Hole with Tara. Nerves are back in full force.

Watching Justin play guitar is worth every minute of primping from Tara and every minute of stress from me.

I tug self-consciously at the stray hairs near my neck. Tara pulled all my hair up, but I have scars back there I'd rather not show off tonight.

Tara suggests we split one of the massive sweet rolls, but just being in here is enough stress for me. Eating would be too much. We're seated way up front, near a window, helping me feel less trapped.

Funny, as I'm sitting here, no one's staring at me. No one's even looking at me. Why do I feel like people must always be staring? I've spent so much time watching the floor that I've never noticed how much they don't look at me. It's a huge relief.

"Hey ya, Kung Fu Girl!" Daisy grabs me from behind.

I jump, but that was her intended purpose, so I don't think I come off as too weird. Fortunately, she lets go of me almost immediately.

"Hey, Daisy." Tara smiles wide.

"Get-together at my place tonight. You girls in?" She wags her eyebrows.

"I'd love a Daisy party, but…" Tara's eyes drift to me.

Right. She came with me and I need to be looked after or something. "I'll find a ride." Which really translates to—I'll call Uncle Rob or Aunt Nicole.

"You're not coming?" Daisy pushes her lower lip into an impressive pout.

"Not this time." The Hole was enough new stuff for me tonight. I shrug. Maybe if I act all cool about not going, sitting this part out won't be a big deal.

The room erupts into applause, and when I look up, Justin is walking toward us.

"Hey, Justin." Daisy stands and pulls him into a hug.

I have to look away. Why is being close to him so easy for her?

"Hey, Daisy." Justin rolls his eyes and smiles at me over Daisy's shoulder.

I smile back even more glad I came than when he was playing.

"You coming to my house tonight?" she asks.

"I'm so not up for a Daisy party." He shakes his head and chuckles.

"Party poopers!" She flits away as fast as she came.

"Are you sure you're okay?" Tara leans in close to me.

"What's up?" Justin asks as he glances between us.

"I wanted to head to Daisy's, but Joy needs a ride home…" Tara raises a questioning eyebrow at him.

"If Joy doesn't mind slumming it with me as her escort, that sounds great." His eyes are on me, sending butterflies spinning in all directions.

"Fine." It squeaks out funny.

"Tell Dad I'll be home at midnight, okay?" Tara squeezes my shoulder, but I can't take my eyes off Justin.

"'Kay."

She bounces out of her seat and runs out the door behind Daisy. Justin takes her seat. "What did you think of the music?"

"Amazing. You two are really good. Your sister sings like an angel."

He chuckles. "I'll tell her. I'm sure she'll get a good laugh out of that."

I have no idea why that's funny.

"You look really pretty." He reaches out like he's going to touch my hair but stops.

I glance down at my black T-shirt and jeans. Poor Tara was pretty disappointed in me. I don't dress girly enough for her.

"Oh. Shoot." He rubs his fingers across his forehead. "I'm still waiting for a car part. Would a walk home be okay?"

"A walk would be even better." Wow, just sitting with him feels like flying.

Justin's sister walks up behind her brother and smiles at me. "You must be Joy."

"That's me."

Her soft face is even prettier up close. "Justin's told me a lot about you."

"Really?" This surprises me. I've hardly said anything to him about myself.

"Well, only 'cause he likes you so much." She pinches his cheek.

My face heats up, which means it's probably red. Now I wish my hair was down to hide me.

"Thank you." Justin flashes his sister an annoyed look, but he's smiling a little, so I'm guessing he's not as annoyed as he seems.

"Better for her to know where you stand." His sister laughs.

I take in her features—dark hair, sweet smile. Her round, pregnant belly is sort of amazing.

She glances down to where I'm looking. "It's something, isn't it?" she asks.

"It's incredible."

"Wanna touch? He's moving around a bit in there." Her voice is so relaxed; she totally doesn't mind.

"What do I...?" But I don't have to worry; she takes my hand and presses it against her belly. She pushes hard, way harder than I'd ever dare to, and then I feel something pushing back against me.

"Wow," I whisper. A baby's in there. I knew this before I touched her. It's just...It really is so miraculous.

"Yeah." Her voice is soft now. "I never get sick of that."

My eyes meet hers. "I wouldn't either."

There's so much love on her face. I bet she'll be a great mother. What a lucky baby. With that thought comes a selfish pang of sadness. Her baby's life will be so different from mine.

"Well, it was nice to meet you, Joy. I'm wiped and heading home." She roughs up Justin's hair before turning away.

"Nice to meet you too," I say.

As soon as she's gone, I realize me and Justin have a long walk ahead of us, and that I'm pretty excited about the time we'll get together. I'm taking huge steps forward.

Justin takes my hand as we walk into the damp night air, our fingers loosely resting together. Neither of us speaks, but I can't stop smiling. I'm proud of myself for one of the first times ever. I've never held a boy's hand before and it feels like this huge deal. But it's Justin, who I like, and I don't feel afraid or anything.

He holds my hand all the way home. We move slowly and our walk is half filled with silence and half filled with him talking. My chest feels all floaty just from having him so close. It's a nice tingling, not the kind that makes me want to run. Our eyes catch often, sending butterflies racing through my insides. As we walk, nothing matters but us. Nothing else exists outside of what we're doing together. The whole walk home. Just me and Justin.

We stand on my porch facing each other.

"I'm glad you came," he says.

"It was fun. You're really good." And I didn't panic or freak out the whole night.

"Maybe we could do it again sometime." His fingers slide over the top of my hand.

My heart's frantic, but in a good way. In a way that makes me feel light, not heavy and dizzy, but like I'm flying again.

He leans forward. His breath is on my face.

I can't breathe. I can't move. I can't swallow.

But I'm okay. We're so close, and I'm okay. I like it.

Him.

His lips touch mine, just briefly, softly.

I step back as I feel the edges of panic itching at my chest. I need to get inside before I panic.

Right now we're good. I just kissed a boy. One I wanted to. One I like.

He steps closer.

His lips push harder this time.

I can't breathe. I'm afraid to move. Flashes of other sets of lips, pushing harder, bodies pushing harder.

Yelling. Holding. Threats. A knife against my throat. I need to get away. Now.

I jerk away, fling open the door to the house, and run inside. My heart bangs in my ears just like it used to when Richard pushed his way into my room.

"Joy?" Justin's voice is quiet. It's late and the house is dark.

I'm already running up the stairs, tears pouring down my face. Memories from my life with Mom are colliding with what I want now, and panic clutches my chest more tightly.

I wanted to kiss Justin and I couldn't. Couldn't stop the thoughts from coming. The memories. The *fear*.

I didn't want to run away, but I did.

I've just lost him. I'm sure of it.

More than I ever have, I hate my mom. *Hate* her and what she did to me—what she let happen to me. I push my way into my room and stand in the center of it, my hands clenched tightly. As the humiliation of how I left Justin on my porch hits me, anger starts to take over.

I throw my fists against the door to my bathroom over and over, making it bang and rattle on its hinges. Each hit sends a wave of pain through my hands, but each loud bang gives me some satisfaction.

"Joy, Joy, Joy, Joy…" Uncle Rob runs into my room in his pajamas. "Shhh…"

Am I screaming? When I stop to look at him, my throat is sore. I didn't hear my screaming, but now I hear the silence. My legs give out from underneath me and I'm sitting, leaning against the doorjamb. My body won't stop shaking.

My hands tremble, I feel numb, but at the same time I hurt everywhere. Like someone has put poison in my veins to split me apart.

Why can't I make the pain stop?

Uncle Rob sits on the floor facing me. His eyes are wide and his breathing is coming fast and hard. "You're okay, Joy. I promise, you're okay."

"I'm not okay!" I shriek. "Are you even in the same room as me?" My breath rasps in ragged bursts. "None of this is *okay!*"

He reaches out for me, but I don't want to be touched, not right now, not by anyone. I jerk away.

I squeeze my eyes tight and let the darkness, pain, and frustration take over.

Richard's face—the stench of him and the horrid feel of his weight on me. It's too hard to fight against right now.

"I'll be right back." Uncle Rob says and I hear him running. He and Aunt Nicole whisper frantically in the hallway.

I let the rest of my body fall onto the floor. It's comforting—lying there with my knees to my chest. Maybe if I can make myself small enough, the poison, the stuff that's splitting me apart, will let me go.

Uncle Rob's on his knees on my floor. "I'm going to pick you up and set you on your bed—is that okay?"

I don't speak. Anything's okay right now. Everything's okay, because *nothing* is okay. I'm relinquishing the control I never had in the first place. His arms carefully scoop me up and he carries me to my bed. He was right to do this. The familiar smell of my sheets and the soft bed underneath me helps me stop shaking. The quivering is just in my hands now, but it still feels like I'm choking on air.

Uncle Rob pulls a chair next to the bed and gently takes my hands. "You're okay, Joy."

"I'm not okay. I don't think there will ever be an end to what she took from me." My body is still doing these weird hiccups as I try to catch my breath.

"I got a special panic-pill for each of us. Because tonight, I need it as much as you." He stuffs a white pill in his mouth and takes a long swallow of water.

"Yeah, like this is totally normal, right?" I take a pill from him and slide it into my mouth, washing it down with the same water.

"Everyone has a different normal, Joy."

I tighten my arms around my legs, and for the first time I'm so grateful for what the pills do for me, taking some of the poison away. Just long enough until I can push it away on my own.

I'm already swimming and my body's relaxed, but my chest hurts from Justin. From how I ran away from him. There are still tears on my face. "How do I make this better?"

"How do I?" Uncle Rob asks.

"You're sharing in my crazy, that's enough." I close my eyes and will myself to go to sleep.

Uncle Rob's hands squeeze mine.

This is what a parent should be. This comfort and sense of strength.

I deserved better.

My mom will never get another piece of me.

Ever.

TWENTY
WEIGHT

There are quiet voices downstairs, which I choose to ignore.

I step into my bathroom and run the cold water in the sink. I'm still breathing, still functioning. But the memory of my night is fresh.

There's a soft knock, and I pause.

"It's Nicole," she whispers, and I open the door.

"Rob had to run into work this morning." Nicole fingers the tattered edge of another one of Rob's T-shirts. "I had to practically shove him out the door."

"Oh." He wanted to stay with me, which is sort of awesome.

"Justin's fine. He said to tell you he's sorry, and that he'll see you on Monday."

I'm such a loser. Why couldn't I just have explained instead of running? Or just…Just backed up and said good night? I probably don't want to know what he thinks of me right now.

"You talked with him?" I ask.

"Just briefly. I happened to be downstairs when you came in."

"Oh." A wave of embarrassment hits me as I think about last night.

"Rob mentioned that you don't like taking your meds. That they make you feel like there's something wrong with you." Her light brown eyes rest on my face. "He took one with you last night to show you that we all need a little help sometimes. Though, with the look on his face, he probably needed it." She chuckles.

"I think I used the word crazy."

"Is that how they make you feel?" she asks.

"How are they *supposed* to make me feel?" How can she not see that taking a pill every day sucks? That having extra super-powerful pills for panic attacks also sucks?

She sits on my bed. "I wish I was better at making you feel better. That I knew what the right thing to say was. I don't. These medicines are tools to keep you healthy, Joy. You wouldn't give it a second thought if you had to take thyroid medicine every day like I do. It keeps my body running normally."

"No." I shake my head. "You and Uncle Rob wouldn't feel the need to carry a little white pill around with you if I wasn't crazy. And if they actually worked, I wouldn't run away from people I really, really like."

Tears rest heavy in my eyes.

"I still stand by what I said about how your pills are tools to keep you healthy."

"Thanks" I say, mostly so she feels like I'm better and will leave. I'm just...I'm not ready to talk and process this all yet. "I need a shower."

She stands up. "See you in a few."

What else am I supposed to say right now?

My shower doesn't make everything go away. The world doesn't feel like a bigger, brighter place because my hair smells like coconuts.

I contemplate going downstairs, but I'm too heavy. It's too far. Instead I curl up in bed again, my wet hair making my pillow damp.

Why did my mom have to be so different from her sister? Was living with me so horrible? Could she not stop drinking for me? Could she not see that I was being hurt? Could she not stop it? Or did she simply not care enough?

There's soft knocking on my door and then it just opens.

"I have McDonald's." Aunt Nicole's voice is soft. "Can I come in?"

"Yeah." But I'm heavy still.

"Do you want to eat?"

"Not really." I can't focus on her. I can't really focus on anything.

"I'm just going to leave this here, and I'm going to check in on you again in a little while."

Right. She'll have to, because I'm the crazy girl. I may be sixteen, but I need to be watched like a toddler. And when I thought I couldn't be heavier, I am.

There are noises downstairs and upstairs. The light from behind my curtain disappears. Good, it's nighttime again, and it'll be less weird that I'm still in bed. A whole day went by. One totally pointless day.

My door cracks open for the…Well, I don't know how many times today someone has opened my door to make sure I'm still here, still breathing.

Uncle Rob sits in the chair from last night.

"I'm just heavy today," I say. "I'm okay." Even the words don't want to come out. When did speaking get so *hard*?

"Lydia wants to see you. I told her to give you a day or two."

How am I supposed to respond to that? *We called your therapist over the weekend. She wants to see you.* It's like confirmation of all my fears. I *am* crazy.

"I can't let you disappear like this, Joy. I can't do it. I'll do anything." His voice sounds like he's crying, but I don't see tears.

Now I feel worse. Uncle Rob is upset because of me.

"How about this. I'll sit here with you tonight on the condition that tomorrow morning you'll get out of bed and get dressed and do something. *Anything.*"

I process his words for a moment. "So the deal is that I'm stuck with you in my room, and my reward is that I have to get out of bed tomorrow?" I ask.

"Is that Joy making a joke?" His face is filled with relief.

Something like another wave of despair crashes into me. "I'm so heavy." I blink and a tear slides down my cheek.

"Then you lean on us for a while. Let us carry you, Joy, until you're not heavy anymore. That's what family is."

I sit silent, trying to process the reality that he cares about me. "I'll try."

He smiles, and I swear it makes him look a thousand times lighter. "That's all I ask."

TWENTY-ONE
TOMORROW

There are a million sayings out there that talk about tomorrow—how you'll see things in a new light, everything will be different, the sun will come out...

The thing is, nothing is different today. I'm still mad at Mom for making me so broken. I still feel like a coward for how I reacted to Justin's kiss. And I still feel like the crazy girl because I couldn't find the strength to get out of bed yesterday.

Today, I think I might be just strong enough to handle one thing. I found someone I really like in Justin, and whatever happened between us is the first thing I want to fix.

Also, my family will feel better because I'm out of bed. So I'm kind of taking care of two things.

How mad is Justin? How insane does he think I am? I picture him again on the small stage behind his guitar, his sister singing next to him.

He sang and played like he felt every note.

I close my eyes and hear the music like I'm there, just like the other night. Justin's fingers dancing on his guitar, and his sister's strong voice.

I need to draw.

Suddenly I'm frantic. I dig through my backpack until I find a pencil and paper.

I start with his hair. Then his shoulders and his arms around his guitar. I'm out of practice. Drawing takes longer than it would have a year ago, but I relax into the feeling of it. I continue to sketch, now with more angles, sharper angles than reality. I like to see the things I draw as fine, smooth, and structured. I sketch out the stage behind him. Then I start his sister with her dark wavy hair and round baby belly.

By the time I'm done, I'm desperate to see him. Talk to him. Apologize to him. Something.

I'm on Justin's doorstep and not really sure what I'm doing or what I think I might accomplish here. All I know right now is that I *miss* him. My hand reaches up and knocks. Crazy how your body can just do things you're not sure you want it to do.

He answers the door. His smile is wide. That's gotta be a good sign. "Joy."

"Would you come walk with me?" I ask.

"Uh…sure." He's blinking and rubs his hand over his hair a few times.

"I want to talk."

He doesn't say anything.

I stare at the porch. "I'm sorry. I really miss you and I'd like to explain if you want to be around me at all. Maybe you don't anymore, and I wouldn't blame you, I just…"

"It's okay, Joy. What happened the other night, I mean. It's okay."

"What?" How can that be? I *ran away* from him.

He tucks his hands into his pockets and straightens his arms, making his shoulders look rigid. "I get it."

"But…" I start. I really thought he'd be mad. I mean, I'd be totally baffled at the very least.

"Why didn't you tell me?"

I'm frozen. My feet, my legs, my body. "Tell you what?" But he doesn't have to answer. Someone told him something. Tara or Aunt Nicole…

"Something about you. Something to make me understand what you need from me. I didn't know…" He has that horrible sympathetic look on his face—the one I got tired of seeing from everyone who came into my hospital room when I was in California. The one it took my aunt weeks to get rid of. I don't want it from him.

My jaw clenches so tight, I'm not sure I'll get the words out. "Didn't know what? Who did you talk to?" I demand.

"Your…Aunt Nicole stepped outside Friday night. She said that you'd lived with your mom your whole life, but she hit you and you didn't get outside, and that…"

"She did *what?*" Every cell in my body is on edge.

"Joy. If you'd told me, I wouldn't have tried to kiss you so soon. I promise I don't care. That's history." But he's not his easy self around me anymore. He's not standing as close as he normally does. I can't catch his eyes, and I feel like he's afraid to look at me. That's not like Justin at all. *How could she…*

"Well, it's my history to share when *I* want to share it." My fists clench up. "I need to talk to my aunt." I spin around and run toward the house.

"Joy! I'm glad I know! I…"

But I don't wait to hear any more.

I jerk open the front door of my aunt and uncle's house. My body's tense with anger from the run home and the thoughts that came with me. I follow Tara's and Aunt Nicole's voices to the dining room and don't get past the doorway before I start yelling.

"You had no right to say anything! None! Talking to Justin was completely unfair, completely intrusive, and there's no excuse for it!" I'm breathing hard, but I feel strong like I do in kung fu. Like I'm in control of this pain, and I can keep it up. I can do it. "I *hate* that you did that! Next time you want to share personal things about me, *don't*!"

I turn out of the room and run upstairs before I feel guilty about the look of shock on Aunt Nicole's face.

I step into my bathroom and stare at my blotchy face in the mirror. I don't care what the family has planned. I don't care that I have homework. Right now I want to hide until this whole mess disappears.

My palms press against my eyes in a lame attempt to keep the tears in as I sit on the toilet, but I cry anyway. This sucks. Things will never be the same with Justin. I'll no longer be the girl who likes silence. I'll be different, tainted. I can't erase what he knows.

Aunt Nicole can't take her words back, and I'm left with another piece of my new life stained by my old one. The one that I'm beginning to think I'll never escape.

TWENTY-TWO
BETTER THAN THERAPY

When I lift my head out of my hands, I'm still on the toilet. Hours I guess, and no one has bothered me. All I want is that strong feeling again.

That's what I'll do. Aunt Nicole won't stop me. Not right now. I change for kung fu and jog out the door. I bring my new phone but don't talk to anyone in the house, don't tell them where I'm going. *This* is freedom.

I run all the way there. Away from the house, and away from the frustration.

"Whatcha doin' here today?" Daisy's smile is wide when I walk in.

"Needed to get out." That's simple enough.

"Problems with the parents?" She looks at me sideways with a smirk and a raised eyebrow. Today her bleached hair is braided into two long braids.

Right. Problems with parents or the people you live with is normal. "Yes."

"Well, the main room is being used for a karate workshop today, but I was about to lift some weights. Come with me. I can spot for you, and you can spot for me."

"Spot?" I'm clueless.

She laughs at my lack of knowledge as I follow her into the weight room, and she gestures to a bench. "Let's get started."

Lifting weights is so different than forcing my body to hold a certain position like in kung fu class. No matter how much I hurt or how determined I am, I just don't have the muscles I need. But each push of my legs on the press gives me some relief, and each strain of my arms on the bench makes me stronger. Daisy changes the weights between me and her. She's been doing this her whole life and lifts a lot more. Occasionally, my phone beeps with new messages, but I'm not ready to deal with them—the messages or the people they might be from.

I'm a sweaty mess, and my arms and legs feel like rubber again, but the workout was all me, and that feels fantastic.

My phone dings again, but I don't answer.

"You know what?" Daisy stops and sets down her weights.

"What?"

"If you keep ignoring the calls, things will just get worse." She gestures to my phone. "Trust me."

"It's different when they're the ones who screwed up." But they cared enough to try and reach me. That's something.

She laughs. "Nope. Parents never think they screw up, just us. I don't care if you don't answer. I'm just saying it'll be less pretty by the hour."

I sigh, climb off the bench, and pick up the phone, checking my texts first.

One from Justin. *I want to see you. What's going on?*

Three from Uncle Rob. *Joy, please call.*

I'm starting to get scared. Please call.

If you don't want to talk send a message so I know you're okay.

Now I feel guilty. I can imagine how torn up he'd be. He didn't want to leave me alone. He sat with me all night and took one of my crazy pills and...I'm almost in tears as I reply.

I'm okay. Sorry. Just mad. Not ready to come back, and hit Send.

"Do you need to get back?" Daisy asks.

"Not right now." I'm not ready to face them. I'm still too angry at Aunt Nicole, and I feel guilty about Uncle Rob.

My phone beeps immediately.

Thank you, Joy. Please call when you're ready to talk or ready for a ride. I promise I'm not mad. Just scared.

It's kind of amazing he admitted that.

I reply: *Need a little more time. I feel better.*

"So, you wanna come back to my house?" Daisy asks.

"I..."

"Come, on Joy. You're looking for a place to be for a while. What do you want to do?" She wags her brows.

"Can I do your hair?" I ask. After spending the day with her, I know exactly what her hair should be like.

"What?" Her eyes get wide. "Isn't that a little girly girl?"

"I think the top of your hair should be black, like near your part."

I point. "And the blond should be underneath. If you want pink, I'm pretty sure I can figure it out." And I know how I'll cut it if she'll let me.

"So, you, uh, know what you're doing, huh?" She walks toward me. I shrug.

"Awesome. Hair it is. Let's ditch this place."

"Daisy! Someone named Tara's here for you!" her mom calls up to Daisy's room.

"Oh." Daisy looks at me. "My guess is she's here for you. Is that okay? Or do you want to hide?"

"It's fine."

"Well, at least you got my hair done." She swishes her head back and forth a few times, laughing.

Daisy looks just like I imagined—black hair on top and around her face, while the bright blond and pink stripes fall from underneath the dark.

"Wow, Joy got you too, huh?" Tara's eyes are on Daisy as she walks in.

"Sorry, Tara," I say. "You didn't need to come searching for me or anything."

Tara shakes her head. "I don't blame you. I get why Mom said something, but she was still out of line. Dad had a fit, though. He was really worried."

Guilt tugs at me and I look at the floor while I gather my thoughts.

"He just worries more 'cause of his…"

"Sister. I know." I stare at my feet. The whole situation sucks because I didn't mean to really hurt any of them. I decide it's stupid that I'm staring at the floor and look at Tara.

"He told you that?" Her eyes are wide.

"I think he wanted me to know why he was so worried about me." There's a moment of silence as Tara and I stare at each other.

"Okay. What's going on here?" Daisy asks.

"Nothing," Tara and I say at the same time.

"So, something you don't want to talk about." She smirks and tosses her hair in front of the mirror a few more times.

"I'm crazy," I tell her. "So they worry about me too much." There. It's an answer suited for Daisy because it's brutally honest.

"I see." She chuckles. "I could have told them that."

"You wanna come home?" Tara asks. "Or…" Her forehead wrinkles in worry.

"Did they send you out after me?" I let out a sigh.

"No. I was worried," she explains. "It didn't take me long to find you, but Justin is worried too."

"Well." I take a step toward the door. "Thanks, Daisy. You're awesome."

"You. Are. Awesome." She throws her arms around me. I hug her back because… Because I guess we're friends.

"Ready?" Tara asks.

"I guess." I wonder how much trouble I'm going to be in…

I text Justin in the car. *I'm found. No worries.* And hit Send.

"*Are* you okay?" Tara asks.

"I'm really sick of people asking that." I pull my feet up onto the seat and stare out the window.

"I know. It's just that I like having you in our house. I mean, if Lydia gets too worried about you, she could…"

"Could what?" My feet are back on the floor and I'm staring hard at Tara with a million possible scenarios running through my head.

"There was talk at first of how maybe you should be in a hospital for a while or something. Mom and Dad begged for you to come to our house."

So they didn't just take me in, they *fought* for me. I'm completely overwhelmed. I slump back in the seat.

"Guess I overreacted, huh?" I ask.

"Umm…I don't know. I don't know your story, and I don't know what Mom told Justin. But she feels really bad about it." Tara bites her lip.

"Thanks." Only now I have a lot more to think about.

TWENTY-THREE
I HAVE NO IDEA IF THIS MEANS I'M MOVING BACKWARD OR FORWARD—MAYBE I'M JUST RUNNING IN CIRCLES

"So, you finally find someone at your school you want to talk to, and it's a boy. Is that right?" Lydia's holding in a smile.

"And Aunt Nicole told him things she shouldn't have." I still ache over the thought of how her words can't be undone.

"And this is why you've missed the last two days of school, and why you won't speak to her, and why your cousin, Tara, is the one that brought you today. Is that right?"

I hate that I read her well enough to hear the disapproval in her voice.

When she puts everything all in the same sentence like that, I sound like I'm totally overreacting. "It wasn't her story to tell."

"I get the impression from her that she told him only what she needed to because she knew you liked him. She thought some of your history would help him understand you, and that maybe he would be more careful in the future." Lydia's normally very good at keeping her voice even, but today I get the impression she's on my aunt's side.

My eyes narrow. "I thought you weren't a message runner between us." Lydia's mentioned a few times that I need to tell my new family my story, not run what I want or need from them through her. It was a serious issue when I first moved in and didn't want to talk to anyone. Lydia refused to be a go-between.

"You need to know her reasons. You won't talk to her. And no, I'm not happy about running messages from her to you." She crosses her arms.

"But she—"

"Then sit down with her and talk about it."

"Fine." Now I cross my arms. So we'll just sit here, arms crossed, and stare at each other.

"Now, I want to talk about Justin."

"And I want to talk about how you wanted me in an institution." I tighten my jaw and force myself to keep my eyes on her.

She takes a deep breath. "I didn't want you in there unless you needed to be. Okay?"

I nod, only partially satisfied.

"Justin."

"What about him?" I ask.

"You're terrified of men, Joy. You don't like your cousin, Trent, and you were scared of your Uncle Rob. All of this is completely understandable, and things you're overcoming. My curiosity here is why are you working toward a relationship with a boy that involves more than friendship?" Her voice is back to the relaxed calm she does so well.

"I..." I don't know. I just like being around him.

"Give that some thought. I'm not saying spending time with Justin is a bad thing, just think a bit about what you're doing, okay?"

"Okay." She's right. I need to talk to Aunt Nicole. I need to talk to Justin. I'm just not sure how, and I *am* still frustrated that a crappy situation between me and Justin turned into this huge mess with my family.

When me and Tara get home, Aunt Nicole sits alone in the dining room. Her hands are folded on the table and she's looking out onto the street.

"Hey." I lean against the doorway.

"Hi." Her eyes meet mine. "Would you come sit?" she asks.

I step in and take a chair at the table with her. "I know you were trying to help. We just never talked about what to say to friends, and..."

"And we should have." She stares down at her hands. "Rob was really upset."

Oh no. "I don't want to cause any problems between you two. That wasn't—"

"No." She holds a hand up. "He was right. Rob and I have learned to work through things over the years. We're totally fine."

"I don't mind you telling people that I used to live with my mom and that because of things she had going on, I had to come here. That's it. No one needs to know more than that." I'm strong. I'm talking with Aunt Nicole and telling her what's okay with me. I have some control.

"I'm so sorry, Joy. It's hard for me to know I hurt you like that."

"Maybe I overreacted. I don't know." Only part of me feels like I overreacted; the other part of me is here because Lydia said I should be. "I felt stupid for running from Justin the way I did."

"What did he...?"

My cheeks heat up and I close my eyes. I'm not sure if I can talk about that.

"I'm sorry," Aunt Nicole says. "That's private. I shouldn't..."

"He kissed me. One small one was okay, but..."

"And then it wasn't. But he's still around. That says a lot about him."

"It does." I nod. It says he's pretty awesome. I want to talk with him next. We've only exchanged texts, and after running away from him not once, but twice, we have a lot to talk about. I just need to figure out what to say.

TWENTY-FOUR
DEFINITELY FORWARD

Kung fu blocks out the stress of facing Justin again. It blocks out Aunt Nicole. Small white pills don't matter. My weaknesses don't matter. All that matters is that I can do this. Tara's next to me today, but she's checking out Brandon more than following stances. I've followed her eyes to that side of the room more than once, and Brandon's smiled at me more than once. Guess he's a nice guy. Tara probably shouldn't be so worried about talking to him.

The familiar burn in my legs isn't as strong as it was when I first started kung fu—I'm really gaining some strength. I stop thinking about Tara and how she likes Brandon, and I don't think about Daisy and how tough she is next to me. I just work. Hard. We're doing blocks now, and I'm fast. Faster than I realized. Daisy may be stronger than me, but she's barely faster—she probably doesn't have as much practice in blocking someone when it really counts.

Class feels longer than normal, but I make it to the end.

"Hey, Joy," Daisy says as we finish up. "A few friends are having a little get together. You remember my house, right? You should come."

"Tonight?" I ask. "It's a school night so I'm not sure how Uncle Rob would feel about me going out."

"What if I promised to have you home by ten?" she asks. Her eyes go to Tara. "You should come too."

Tara's eyes are elsewhere. "Yeah, maybe."

"What's going on over here?" Uncle Rob asks. Brandon and Trent step up behind him.

"I was hoping that Joy could come hang at my house for a bit tonight," Daisy says.

"Uh..."

"We'll all go," Brandon rests his arm over Trent's shoulder. "Keep an eye on Joy." He winks at me.

I look at Uncle Rob. I'd rather not be winked at when I don't know what Brandon could mean by it.

"Yeah." Tara nods, steps closer, and smiles at Brandon. "We'll all go."

"I guess." Uncle Rob gives us each a stern look. "I'll be by to pick you up at ten."

Wow. I feel so...free. "Okay, yeah, great." And then I remember that Daisy is sort of famous for her parties, and I wonder what I'm in for.

Uncle Rob leans into me. "I'll slide a pill in your coat pocket. Keep your phone on you and call if you need anything, okay?"

"'Kay." I feel a little like I'm being watched too carefully, but more like I'm *free*. And free in the good way—meaning I'm out and doing something with friends, and my aunt and uncle know where I am, and no one's mad at anyone else like they were when I disappeared the other day.

"I'll be outside Daisy's house at ten. If you don't want me knocking on the door or wandering through the yard calling your names"—he points to Tara and then to Trent—"be outside."

This is it. We're going to a Daisy party.

Tara and I ride with Daisy. Trent and Brandon take Brandon's car. Tara fiddles with her hair the whole time and mumbles about how she wishes she wasn't sweaty.

I sit quietly in the back while Daisy screams the lyrics to a song that makes no sense and hurts my eardrums. I don't mind the singing though. It seems like such a Daisy thing to do that I soak up her happiness.

We pull into the driveway, and I climb out of the car. Her yard is so different at night.

Despite how dark the sky is, the fire and lights in the house illuminate sections of the massive lawn. Scattered trees run along a tall privacy fence that stops where the lake starts. I stare out at the water and the small reflections of yellow light from the other houses on shore.

Daisy grabs my hand and walks with me toward the fire.

I don't know if holding her this tight is good or bad, but sticking close to someone I trust is what I know to do.

"Hey, Joy." Brandon laughs as he runs up behind us. He rests a hand on my shoulder.

I spin to look at him, Daisy's hand still firmly grasped onto mine.

"Watch out for Daisy—she has a cunning ability to make people do things they don't want to do." He winks at her, smiles at me, and moves away. "If you need someone to watch out for you, I'm your guy."

"He totally likes you," Daisy whispers as we stop near the fire. She picks up a cup and takes a long drink.

I recognize the smell on Daisy's breath, alcohol for sure, but not beer. I'm okay with anything that's not beer.

"Well..." That sucks. It would be much simpler if he liked Tara. "I don't like him, so..." I shrug.

Daisy laughs. "My guess is that you're the only girl here who doesn't."

Weird.

There are about fifty people our age scattered between the house and the fire pit, and I'm not the most comfortable I've ever been, but the party is no more startling and new than my first few days at school. If I can channel the tough girl from kung fu class, I'll be fine.

"Let's jump into the lake!" Daisy grabs my shoulders with her hands.

I stare at the large black hole that is her lake.

"No." I shake my head. The only light out there comes from the few houses on the shore, and the whole scene—with the dark trees, black lake, and lawn lit by campfire— looks like the beginnings of a horror movie.

"Come *on*, Joy. No one ever does it with me." She pouts.

Can I admit this? I lean toward her so no one else hears. "I can't swim."

"It's okay," she whispers back. "We'll use life jackets. Easy. They'll make us float."

Easy. Right. My heart pumps faster and I'm actually considering following her, which is crazy. Completely insane, but I'm *choosing* if I want to or not—and that makes all the difference.

"Channel that kick-ass girl I know you are." Her smile is wide. She drags me toward a small cabin near the dock. "For as much time as you can hold a horse pose, you can totally do this."

"Isn't it freezing out here for this kind of thing?" I ask, but maybe she's right. Maybe I am tough enough for this. That would really be something.

"We're tough girls. We kick ass." She laughs. "Just hold your breath when you go under and then kick your legs until your head pops back out of the water." She hands me a life jacket.

Best to just jump in before I think too much. Probably.

I'm shaky but determined. Hold breath, kick, breathe again. I chant this over and over in my head as I buckle the life jacket. I can do horse stance. I can do this. I can do bow stance. I can do this. I can block. I can do this. I can be in kung fu and keep up. I'm so doing this.

"We're going in!" Daisy yells the direction of the campfire. "Any of you wimps joining us?"

A few kids laugh and come our way. They're all just shadows

with the bonfire behind them lighting up their silhouettes.

Her eyes, wide with excitement, meet mine. "Come on. You ready?"

I can only nod. I'm going to do something I've never done, and I'm afraid, but I'm going to burn through the stress and jump into the dark lake at the end of the dock.

I'm stronger than my fear. Stronger than my fear...

A second small wave of panic sets in as we near the dock. I push it away. I'm tough enough to push it away. Strong enough. I stand at the edge of the dock with one foot still on the lawn, looking at the rows of wood boards between me and the water. My heart's beating so loud that it drowns out almost everything else.

"Best to run and get it over with. I'll hold your hand." Daisy's jaw is set.

"No way you girls will go through with it!" A guy yells from behind us.

"That's our cue." Her eyes narrow, and I see the face of determination she wears in kung fu. It's a mix of tight-jawed tough girl and mischievous smirk that probably only someone like Daisy could pull off.

Yeah. I can do this. *I'm stronger than my fear.*

Daisy starts to run, and I run with her. We're tough girls. I grasp her hand in a death grip.

We run past the lights on the side of the dock and the black water gets closer and closer. I falter once as the reality of jumping into a lake when I can't swim hits me again. But I'm stronger than that. Stronger than the dark. Stronger than the cold. Than the water. Than my fear.

I'm in control of this. I can do this. My legs push me forward, the boards make a rumbling, clacking noise underneath our feet, and then we're flying off the end of the dock into the air.

I did it.

I scream as I hit the icy water. It pricks every inch of skin and steals my breath. I kick my legs as hard as I can and let the life jacket pull me to the surface. Just like Daisy promised, my head pops out into the air.

My laugh is loud, excited. I'm shivering, but I did it. I made myself shiver. I made myself jump. *I have power to make things happen.*

"You're awesome, Joy!" Daisy throws her arms around me, and I sputter as the weight of her lowers me in the water.

"Get me to the dock! I'm freezing!" I laugh and spit lake water out of my mouth. And then I yell in excitement with the rush of what I just did. Amazing.

She swims us to the ladder. I kick awkwardly, paddle my arms, and grab the rails to pull myself up. I *am* a tough girl.

A hand reaches down and I take it to help on the last step. When I stand up, I come face to face with Brandon. It's so surprising to have him this close I nearly take a step back and end up in the lake again.

He grabs my elbow, keeping me upright, and he's chuckling. "I told you Daisy was trouble."

I open my mouth to say something, but nothing comes out because Justin's walking up the dock, and the excitement and relief at seeing him pushes away everything else.

He's the guy I've run away from two times in a row, but I can't take my eyes off his shape moving toward me. I want to yell and throw my arms around him but instead I keep staring.

"You're so awesome!" Daisy attacks me from behind as she stands up on the dock. "No one ever jumps with me. *Ever!*"

"I've jumped with you." Justin laughs as he comes to a stop in front of us, glancing more than once at Brandon, who's still standing too close.

"Once." She rolls her eyes. "More than a year ago, when you were still *fun*." She puts an arm over my shoulder. "Come on. You can borrow my clothes."

"Uh…" Jumping in a cold lake I can do. Changing clothes in front of Daisy? That I can't do. "I'm headed home in a bit anyway, I'll just stand by the fire to warm up."

She laughs. "Well, I'm freezing my ass off. I'll be back out in a sec."

I stare at my feet, even though my body's starting to shiver. Nobody says anything, but Brandon follows Daisy off the dock, and I take a deep breath of relief. Brandon liking me would be really inconvenient.

The group that wandered toward the lake is heading back to the fire, and instead of worrying about being alone with Justin, I'm relieved.

"I can't believe you did that."

I can just make out his crooked smile in the dark.

I'm even more proud of myself than I was a moment ago because the reality of what I just did is really starting to sink in. "Yeah, well, I'm a tough girl now." I clutch the life jacket and my body shivers, but the shivering is something I did to myself. That makes all the difference.

"You've always been a tough girl." He swings his body toward the shore. "Let's get you near the fire so you can get warm."

Another round of shivers shakes my body, and I hold my arms like that'll miraculously smooth down my goose bumps.

"You're friends with Brandon?" he asks as we walk. But his voice sounds weird. Like something's wrong.

"I don't know him. He's Trent's friend, but he seems nice. Tara really likes him." It's hard to talk because my teeth are chattering. I'm not sure if the fire will be enough to warm me up.

"You've got to be freezing."

"I am." I nod but then laugh. "Because I jumped in a lake. Did you know I can't swim?"

He shakes his head a little, his smile spreading even wider. "I didn't know that."

I let out a breath and look behind me at the blackness of the lake. Only two people jumped off tonight and I was one of them. "That was amazing. Seriously amazing."

"Good." He frowns as my body convulses in another round of shivering. "I'm wearing two shirts. How about I give you one so you have something dry on top?"

"Where will I change?" I look around. We're outside in the dark. Nothing but lawn and campfire.

"I'll watch the door of the boathouse." He jerks his chin in the direction of the small cabin.

Justin opens the door for me, tugs off the long-sleeve shirt he's wearing, and I step inside. It's so dark I can barely see the walls. I stand, cold and soaked, with Justin's T-shirt in my hand. My stiff fingers fumble with the life jacket buckles. I'm not sure if I'm ready to be half naked in here.

"You okay?" Justin asks from outside.

"Yeah. Just a sec." Now I have to laugh at myself. I just jumped into a freezing lake, without knowing how to swim, and now I'm afraid to change. I rip off my wet T-shirt and slide on Justin's. It smells like him and still has his warmth. Suddenly he feels closer to me. Like we're next to each other.

My kung fu shorts are dripping wet, freezing, and clinging to my legs, but I don't mind. *I just jumped into a lake.* This makes me strong. Powerful. Awesome.

Justin and I sit on Daisy's front porch, waiting for Uncle Rob. My wet T-shirt sits on the ground in front of me, and a towel from the house is wrapped around my legs and wet shorts.

"I'm sorry for..." Justin starts.

I shake my head. "No. Don't be sorry for anything. I have enough sorry from my aunt and uncle to last me lifetimes."

He clasps his hands together. "I don't want you to be mad at your aunt. She was trying to help."

"Well…I wasn't ready to say anything. She took that away from me." I tighten the towel around my legs for something to do.

"Well, I'm glad she did. I mean, I'm not glad because of you, but I'm glad that I know, because I thought I'd completely blown my chance with you." His body leans toward me so slightly that I'm not sure he moved at all.

"I don't know how to explain what living with my mom was like, and I don't think I'm ready to. Not yet. But it's awkward for me…I mean, I have a hard time with men…being around them and stuff." My heart races, but I'm determined to continue. "And me having a hard time with that…has to do with my mom not, um, not protecting me from them…at certain times." I can't *believe* I got that out.

"I'm sorr—"

But I silence him by holding up my hand, and I actually smile.

"I'm not really a man." The teasing that I love is in his voice again. "I mean, I'm barely seventeen. I'm only a junior in high school. And I'm not a big guy. So I don't think I fall into that category."

His smirk eases some of the tension, but I can't find any more words right now.

"This is hard, 'cause I don't want to scare you away," Justin says, "but I want you to know how I feel." He pauses, sliding his fingers over his watch strap. "I don't like any other girls. And since there are no other girls I really want to hang out with, I'd like to hang out with you."

170

The words float between us as I fight to find something to say. "But what if I can't...I mean, what if we start, and then I freak out, or I still don't work right, or..." There are a million ways I could screw this up. I rest my chin in my hands and stare at my feet, determined to find the strength I just felt with Daisy.

Justin crosses his legs and he leans back. "I like being around you. In silence, in non-silence, whatever. If you get sick of me, let me know so I can back off. But I wanna stick around."

"But..."

"Joy, maybe you don't like me the way I think you do, or maybe you don't want to hang out with anyone." He scoots closer. "I'm just looking for a friend, that might—"

"A friend that might lead to more." I rest my cheek on my hand so I can see him to try to read his face so I know what he's thinking.

"But only when you make the move."

"Oh, so really, this is just a ploy to make sure that I don't run away from you again. And that I'll have to be the one to put myself out there to move forward?" I smirk.

"Is Joy teasing me?" He chuckles.

"A little." I'm lighter. Just with our conversation. With giving him some of my history.

"Well, you're right. But I'm putting myself pretty far out there too. The thought of making you uncomfortable...that just sucks. So, yeah. You tell me when you want to hold my hand or when you want to *kiss* me..." He smirks. "Because eventually you'll want to kiss me."

"Well, don't you two look cozy." Daisy plops herself next to me in an oversized set of sweats. She slides her arm through mine and rests her head on my shoulder. "Most people don't get me, Joy. But you do."

"I don't get you at all." I rest my head on hers.

"Justin's a nice guy. He's been a good friend of mine for a long time. He was my first kiss."

I suddenly feel like I'm in the middle of two people I shouldn't be in the middle of. Were Justin and Daisy together? But they're not now, so why does their possible history make me feel like I don't want to be here anymore?

"That's great, Daisy," Justin says. "Way to add some awkward into the convo. How much have you had to drink tonight?" he asks.

"Just a couple of shots. That's all." She makes a face.

"Just enough to drag Joy into the lake." He leans forward to look at Daisy.

"She ran with me, Romeo." Daisy's eyes widen.

"My uncle's here." I stand up. "I gotta go." I don't look back. Just walk toward Uncle Rob's car.

"Wait, Joy, I think you…" Justin starts.

"'Night, Justin." I wave at him. "Thanks for the swim, Daisy." I open the car door.

"Can I call you later?" Justin asks.

"It's late. I'll see you tomorrow." But I don't look at him, and I'm not even sure why. I'm just…It's all suddenly confusing—just when I got my feelings straightened out.

"You're wet." Uncle Rob stares as I climb in the car.

"Oh, your car. I'm so sorry." I try to pull myself off the seat, but there's nowhere to go.

"I'm not worried about the car, Joy. How did you get wet?"

I smile wide. "I ran off Daisy's dock. It was amazing." The exhilaration of flying through the air and hitting the cold wall of water hits me again. I'm brave.

Uncle Rob's jaw drops. "I...Do you know how to swim?"

"Nope. And I jumped anyway." It feels huge.

"I'm not sure what to say." But there's a smile tugging on the corners of his mouth. He's proud of me, which feels almost as good as the jump. "Where are Tara and Trent?" he asks.

"No idea."

He lays on the horn just as they run around the corner of the house.

Tara climbs in the back without a word. Trent waves to Uncle Rob, points toward the road, and starts walking up the driveway.

Justin is still standing there, watching me through the window. I wave, and he waves back. A perfect, simple gesture to end our evening.

Uncle Rob starts to back out of the driveway and rolls down his window. "Get in the car, Trent."

"*Joy*." Trent widens his eyes at me. "Doesn't like the smell of beer."

"You were *drinking?*" Uncle Rob's driving slowly and Trent's walking alongside the car.

"One beer, Dad. It's not a big deal." Trent shrugs as he walks.

"It is to me. We'll talk later." Uncle Rob rolls his window back up. I've never heard his voice that tense.

I rub my hands up and down on my wet shorts, hoping for some warmth.

"Did you have fun, Tara?" Uncle Rob asks.

"I guess." But Tara's whisper barely carries from the backseat.

"Wait." Uncle Rob's eyes scan me again. "Where did you get the dry shirt?"

Oh. Right. The story might sound weird. "It's Justin's, but he had a shirt on under this shirt, and I changed somewhere private. It's not…I mean, it's no big deal." I shake my head.

"I didn't know you'd invited Justin."

"I didn't. He and Daisy are friends." The weirdness of Justin and Daisy pricks at me again.

"And what are you and Justin? Or should I not ask that?" His hands grip the steering wheel a little more tightly.

"We're…It's all really confusing," I admit.

He chuckles. "Well, relationships being confusing is something that won't change for a while."

"Oh." That's not very comforting.

"I just wanted to make the point that some things are complicated for everybody."

"Thanks." I breathe in the smell of Justin's shirt again. It smells like a citrus-scented laundry detergent and something else that's all him. I suddenly wish I'd told him to call tonight.

TWENTY-FIVE

STRAIGHTENING THE CONFUSION? OR MAKING IT WORSE?

I leave the house alone the day after my first Daisy party, still a little high from the feeling of jumping off her dock.

Tara rode with Trent, which is weird because he just started dating a different girl, and I know she's tired of him being with so many people. But I spot Justin at the end of the driveway and suddenly I'm glad Tara rode with her brother.

"Hey there," Justin says as soon as I reach him.

"Hey," I squeak, still feeling a bit raw and exposed after telling him what I did last night.

"I want to talk, Joy." His voice is low, making him sound more serious than I'm used to.

We slow down until I'm barely shuffling.

"I'm glad I got to see you last night," he says.

"At Daisy's," I say stupidly.

He shrugs. "I used to party with that group a lot. All last year. I don't anymore. Not often. A week night seemed like a good night to touch base with all those friends again."

"Why not anymore?" I ask.

"It just stopped being fun. That's all."

"And you and Daisy." I watch our feet for a few steps. "I didn't know..."

"Daisy and I are *just* friends, and only sort-of friends. I mean, she's a cool girl, I've known her forever, but she has the attention span of a hamster."

I laugh. "What does that mean?"

"It means she's nice, but hard for me to be around. I may be ADD, but I don't hold a candle to her. It's just...the way she said things last night. I thought you might have gotten the wrong idea." His hands are in his pockets, and he slants his body toward mine as he speaks, making me feel like he might want to be closer still.

"I'm not upset or anything. I mean, we're not..." Why can't I just tell him I like him, but that he shouldn't feel trapped with me because I don't know how to be with someone the way he wants to be?

"I thought we were past you not understanding how I feel about you." His voice is almost a whisper, and I feel like I've hurt his feelings. "I like you. You're the girl I want to hang out with, and if it leads to more that would be great. If it doesn't...This is still where I want to be."

My heart thumps harder with his honesty. This can be like jumping in the lake. Maybe being around him will be less scary if I take control. Isn't that what we decided last night anyway?

I let out a breath and reach my hand to take his. His fingers are warm and the closeness of him feels…My knees go weak it's so good.

I can hold his hand. I can let go. Things can happen when *I* want them to because he's okay with that.

"You're smiling," he says, giving my hand a squeeze.

I should be able to look at him now. I pull my head up and our eyes meet. "Yep."

"Thanks, Joy"—he bumps his shoulder against mine—"for giving us a chance."

"Thanks, *Justin*," I tease. I don't want to be treated differently. Well, I guess I do, but I don't want it to *feel* like I'm treated differently.

"Can we get together later?" he asks.

"I have kung fu." With how Justin and I are moving forward and how I'm barely back in good with my family after disappearing, I need kung fu right now.

"So, you're the smart girl, which is hot. And now you're the kung fu girl, which is also hot."

My cheeks heat up.

"That's kind of awesome. Would it be weird if I stopped by?"

"It's sort of the thing I do with my dad—I mean, with Uncle Rob and Trent."

"Okay." His voice is all relaxed.

He seems totally okay with me saying no. I can do that. I can say no, and we'll still be fine.

"If you want to call him Dad, why don't you?" I love how Justin just puts everything out there.

"He's not…" I stammer. "I mean, they're not my parents. They already have two kids and…"

"And?" He pauses to stare at me. "I bet they'd love it."

"Maybe." My heart fills to bursting at the thought.

"Thanks for letting me walk with you," he says as we start across the school parking lot.

"I can't believe how good you are at this."

"This what?"

"Just…" I squeeze his hand. "This. You know. Talking."

"Oh." He kicks a stray rock under a car. "Dad insisted we all go to counseling when Mom wanted to leave. And then more after she left. He was worried, that's all. Once you get in that habit of keeping things in the open, it sticks with you."

"I didn't know your mom left. I'm sorry." Feeling bad for him because his mom left is so foreign. I spent nights praying my mom would leave. Guess his mom didn't want him either, just in a different way. A way that let him go, instead of keeping him trapped.

I'm honestly not sure which is worse.

Trent has a girl backed against the lockers. He's touching the side of her face and she's eating it up, but the look on his face is one I recognize, and it isn't one she should be happy about.

I'm glad I didn't see him like this when I first moved in. He would have scared me even more.

"Trent?" I call out, but I know I might be too quiet even though the halls are practically empty.

His shoulders slump before he looks my way. "What?" His voice is impatient, annoyed.

"I'm walking home, and Tara has a ride." I have to clear my throat to continue. "I just wanted to let you know."

"Fine." He eyes leave mine and go back to the girl in front of him. He whispers, but I can still hear. "Looks like I have the car to myself. Want a ride home?"

She giggles as he puts his arm around her waist.

I turn and walk away, wishing I knew him better so that I could talk to him about the possessive way he looks and holds the girls he's with. But really, what would I say?

Tara and I sit on the floor of my room with our after-school snack. Aunt Nicole bought Oreos, and we've taken the whole bag. I'd never had an Oreo before but now they're my favorite.

"So how are things with you and Justin?" She stares at the cookie in her hand.

I frantically chew and swallow another bite so I can answer. "I don't know. I think good. I like being around him." My face turns hot at the thought.

"And what about…" I hear her suck in a deep breath. "Brandon?"

"I don't like Brandon. You like Brandon." He's not even on my radar except that I know Tara likes him. I grab another cookie and stuff the whole thing in my mouth—it's the easiest way to make sure I get the right amount of all the parts.

"It doesn't matter." She nibbles her Oreo as if she's only allowed to eat one and is trying to make it last forever.

I chomp a few more times before I'm able to answer. "Well, it *does* matter. If he doesn't like you, then you should like someone else."

She laughs. "Just like that, huh?"

"Wouldn't it be easier?" I ask.

"I love you, Joy." She puts her arms around me. "Of course it would be easier, but things don't always work the easy way. You should know that."

A subtle weight rests on my shoulders. I do know that.

"Another cookie?" She holds one out to me.

"Definitely."

I guess even though Brandon maybe likes me, Tara and I are okay.

TWENTY-SIX
BOYS

The fire is lit in the den. The door is open—the rule when I have a guy over. The bizarre thing is that I like the rules. They mean someone's watching out for me. I'm well aware that I'm probably the only sixteen-year-old who doesn't mind strict guardians.

Justin's fingers move easily up and down his guitar, and I love his face in this state of concentration. He stops and folds his arms over the top, drops his chin on his hands, and rests his eyes on me.

"Why did you want to talk to me?" I ask.

"What are you talking about?"

"When we first met on the sidewalk, you said you'd wanted to talk to me since I came to school but were afraid to. Or something like that."

"You were quiet, didn't look at anyone, but I could see in your eyes that you were thinking. A lot. I wanted to know what you were thinking about."

His answer is more profound than I expected. "I've been holding on to something I did for you." I reach into my back pocket for the drawing I did of him and his sister. It's creased since it's been tucked in there for a while.

"Really?" He sets his guitar aside, and I hand the drawing to him.

He unfolds the paper and stares.

"You did this?" His eyes are wide. "You put me to shame."

"No!" That's the opposite of my intention. "We have different styles, that's all. I'm all angles."

"I draw all the rounder edges when you find all the angles." He's still studying the drawing. "I didn't know you drew."

"No one knows. Well, my mom knows." Me telling Justin something about myself I haven't told anyone from my new life feels like a giant leap to being as close to him as I think I want to be. "This was the first time I felt like drawing in a long time. I want to do one for everyone here, but I don't know if they'll get it. Me. You know, my style, or if the drawings would just be silly." Even the thought of doing something so personal makes me want to fold up into myself.

"They wouldn't think it's silly." His eyes are still on the sketch.

"I've held on to it for a while."

"Do you have pictures from when you lived with your mom?" he asks.

"The police have those. I drew some of the people she had over and…" I'm about to reveal too much information.

"You don't have to say anything, Joy. It's okay." He looks at me over the picture.

I stare at the fire, more blue tonight. "Some of the people Mom brought over were worse than her, and she never really did anything to stop them." I let out a breath of air. Giving information about my past is getting easier. Slowly.

His fingers reach out for mine, and he laces our hands together. "Thank you. You know, for sharing. You're good for me."

"I'm *good* for you?"

"It's like...calm around you. That's good for me."

"Really?" Because I feel stressed out most of the time.

"I guess I look at what you've done after a tough past, and I feel like a prick for being a jerk the last couple of years."

I stare at our hands together. Such a simple thing that feels so good. "Thanks for listening." *And still being here, even though I'm still crazy, may always be crazy. And even though all I can bring myself to do is hold your hand when I'm pretty sure you'd like another kiss.*

TWENTY-SEVEN
BACK TO THE LISTS

Reasons Joy isn't crazy—

- *She can sort of keep up with Daisy sometimes*
- *She does kung fu in a room full of men who are learning martial arts and they're all loud*
- *She talks to Justin, holds his hand, and shared a little bit of her past with him*
- *She's drawing again*
- *She's falling in love.*

TWENTY-EIGHT
NOT SURE YET

The tall blond guy who's a friend of Trent is staring at me. The guy from the mall. The one who stuck his face in my face. Right now I'm loving my pink-slip status because I stand up and walk out of class four minutes before the bell.

I pull in a few deep breaths the second I step into the quiet halls. I'm okay.

I roll through my locker combo and pull it open. Now I have something else to think about—books, messy locker, homework…

"I don't really appreciate the fact that I'm not allowed to go to Trent's house anymore." His words snake up my spine and I glance around the edge of the small door. It's blond guy. And no one else is here.

I'm shaking and lean into my locker as if the small door can offer protection. I know he's walking toward me, even though I'm afraid to look. I didn't know Trent's friends weren't allowed over anymore.

"Still silent?" His voice lowers as he gets closer.

Why can't I just run away? Isn't that the simplest solution?

"What are you so afraid of?" I can feel the heat from his body behind me.

I'm weak. Trembling. All I want is for my legs to keep holding me up. Where *is* everyone? Why won't the bell ring so we won't be alone in the hall?

I see his hand against the locker next to mine. "Watch yourself, little girl."

The bell finally rings, and I jump. I feel him move away and lean into my locker for support. I'm gasping for air. I have to find a way to get myself under control. He's just some dumb kid. But he's so much bigger than I am. I carefully wipe my tears as the hall becomes busy with students. Just a few more deep breaths, and I'll be—

"Hey."

I jump at the sound of Justin's voice, and try to smooth my hair with shaking hands.

"What's going on with you?" he asks.

I turn and his forehead is pinched in worry, a slight frown pulls at the corners of his mouth.

"Uh…nothing. I'm fine." But I know my voice comes out strange. Even with my heart whooshing in my ears, I know I don't sound right.

"Joy, you're shaking. What happened?" He starts to reach out for me but stops.

"I told you I don't work right," I snap.

"Can I walk home with you today?" he asks.

"I just want to be alone." But I also want to be with him. What do I say so I don't hurt his feelings?

He takes a breath and rubs his forehead.

Now I should apologize. It's not his fault I'm so inept. "I'm sorry."

"No, it's cool, right? I said it's okay." He stuffs his hands in his back pockets and steps back.

"Thanks." I stand at my locker and feel a sharp pang of sadness as he walks away. Why do I have to be such a mess over this?

Trent's home when I walk in, glaring at me from the kitchen as I come in the door, and setting cold fear in my gut. I run upstairs to the quiet of my room and lock the door.

It's dark. Black. I wave my hands in front of my face but can't see them. It's hard to breathe. Almost impossible. Someone grabs me in the dark, but I break free and run away. Faster, faster my legs push. I can make it out. I can do it. The darkness fades and my heart sinks when I see where I am. The house that holds me. The dingy white walls. The familiar smell. No, I scream. Please, no!

And I push harder, push longer, my legs keep moving. I'm almost to the door. Almost there. A hand on my ankle pulls me to the ground. The blond guy from school appears next to me just before I scream.

I wake up half panicked, half resigned. As soon as I hear my door crack open I flip over my pillow. "I'm fine," I say as I lie back down, facing the wall—even though I'm anything but.

Aunt Nicole sighs behind me. At this point my nightmares make me feel stupid and weak, which is almost worse than afraid. I'm waiting for her to step back out of my room, but she doesn't.

My bed bends with the weight of her, and her voice comes out in a whisper. "If you need me to leave, I'll go. But I don't want to."

I don't move. My head's on my pillow, and I relax with the warmth of her hand running up and down my back. Each gentle movement makes me relax more, spreading warmth through me. Tears come, but they're tears of disbelief and gratitude. This woman pulled me into her family like I never expected, like I'd never have let myself hope. I will never, ever, be able to repay her.

"I'm glad I ran into you," I say the second I see Justin coming up the street.

I stand at the end of the driveway and wait for him to catch up.

"I was worried. You didn't answer my texts," he says.

Right. Because I wasn't sure what to tell him about how I reacted yesterday at school.

Tara and Trent pull out of the driveway in their car, and I watch them drive away.

"Why don't you ride with them?" he asks.

I shrug. "I do sometimes."

"But not today." He smiles. "Is it okay that I'm standing here, sort of hoping you wanted to walk with me?"

"I do want to walk with you." We stand in silence for a moment, but I still have a lot I want to say. "I didn't know what to say to you. That's why I didn't answer. Sorry about yesterday." I'm determined to be strong. To be the tough girl. I step closer to him and then closer still and give him a soft hug.

His arms reach only kind of around me and rest on my shoulders, his thumbs softly rubbing the tension from my arms. "This is nice." His warm breath hits my neck and sends shivers through me. Intense. "Being close to you. Really. Really. Nice."

"Yeah." I step back and immediately miss the warmth of him. "We ready?"

"Of course." He reaches his hand out and I take it. So the beginning of my day is already looking better than yesterday.

Blond guy is in three of my classes. How could I have missed that?

He sits down in Justin's chair before the bell rings for government.

I try to ignore him and stick my face in my book. I've done nothing to him. I don't understand why he doesn't leave me alone.

"I know you see me, Joy." His voice may be low as a whisper, but it's meant to scare. I know that tone well.

"Excuse me." Justin stands between us. He looks taller, bigger than he normally does. "You're in my seat."

"Right. Whatever." Blond guy stands up and walks slowly back to his chair.

"Are you okay?" Justin leans over. "What was that about?"

Think, think, think. "He's uh, a friend of Trent's, and was just saying hi." The last thing I need is Justin seeing another way I'm weak, or added drama with the people around me.

Justin touches my hand.

I jump.

"I don't believe you."

"I…" I let my eyes find his.

"You don't have to share. I just want to make sure you're okay," he whispers as the teacher starts class.

I nod because I don't know what else to do. Being the victim of blond guy's attitude isn't something I want to talk about or admit right now. I reach across the aisle, glad we're in the back row, and take his hand.

He gives me a light squeeze.

For the first time, Justin's touch helps my heart slow and my body relax.

TWENTY-NINE
IT ONLY LOOKS LIKE OVERREACTION—WELL, AND SORT OF FEELS LIKE IT TOO

"I just don't see why I can't change my mind and do home-school again." I'm staring at Uncle Rob and Aunt Nicole across the table. Anything to avoid school. To avoid the blond guy who makes me feel like the weak girl I don't want to be anymore.

"Where is this coming from?" Uncle Rob asks.

"Nowhere," I insist. "It's just what I want to do."

Aunt Nicole and Uncle Rob exchange glances.

Aunt Nicole speaks. "Joy, something's going on. Please just tell us what it is."

"Nothing's going on!"

"Why don't you take a…a day off tomorrow?" Uncle Rob suggests. "And we'll talk about it again later. There's more going on here, and we need to know what it is before we can make any kind of decision."

I slump in defeat. I bought myself one day, and then what?

THIRTY
SANITY DAY

"I'm taking my sanity day with you." Tara flops down next to me in front of the TV.

"Sanity day?" I ask.

"Yeah, that's what Mom and Dad call it when you just need a day off."

"Oh." I can guess why they didn't use that term with me. But it's nice to know that Tara needs one once in a while too. And that means I can take a day off, and it won't be a big deal. "Why did you take a day?"

"It's just..." She sighs. "Camilla is the only friend from last year who still talks to me outside of school, and I don't know why no one else does. And every girl Trent has dumped this year has made a point to tell me what a jerk my brother is. Or I get a bunch of girls asking if I can introduce them to him. And Caitlynn, his girlfriend from last year is still so nice to me, and it just makes me feel guilty even though I shouldn't because I didn't dump her. Being a twin sucks."

"And then Brandon. I'm really sorry. I didn't…"

"You didn't do anything wrong, Joy. I promise, we're fine." But she looks so…defeated. I miss her smile.

"Sorry." It's dumb to say it again, but it's all I have.

"It's nothing like what you're facing, I'm sure."

"Just different." Can I tell her? Maybe the whole situation isn't a big deal. "One of Trent's friends keeps harassing me."

"Is that why you're home?" She leans forward.

I nod.

"Tyler? The blond guy?" she asks.

"How did you know it was Tyler?"

"Justin and I have sixth period together. He asked me if I knew what was going on with Tyler 'cause he saw him talking to you, and you seemed upset. We both know you don't like to talk to people, so it didn't seem too strange, but Tyler's a jerk, so we weren't sure."

"You guys were talking about me?" Without me?

"Joy, we're family. We watch out for each other. It's what friends do. It's what family should always do. That's all." She's smiling.

"I guess." Is it normal for people to go out of their way to watch out for me?

"So…" She grins. "Justin really likes you."

"He's sweet, I'm just sort of…" Talking needs to get easier for me because it's like my tongue has swollen up. "I feel…nervous around him…sometimes."

"Joy, I've never had a boyfriend—not for more than a week or for dates at dances. Trent pretty much scares everyone off. If I had a guy as into me as Justin is into you, I'd be all nervous about being around him, you know?" She slides deeper into the couch.

Tara makes me feel better, but I'm still not sure if I believe her. Relationships seem so easy for everyone else. I think of the easy way Daisy grabbed Justin in a tight hug. And even after weeks of talking with him, I'm not there yet.

Our day passes in movies that Tara's shocked I haven't seen. They're all very romantic and completely unbelievable, but she seems to be smiling more than she was this morning. I have a little better understanding of friends and relationships, I feel closer to Tara, and I got some Oreos. Sanity days might be my favorite.

It's late but I can't sleep. Taking a pill would be okay with me, but I don't want to wake Aunt Nicole and Uncle Rob to get it. Anyway, sometimes normal people can't sleep. My day off helped, but I still have to go to school tomorrow. I roll onto my stomach and rest my head on my arm. On Justin's shirt. The one I hope he doesn't want back.

I think about how Aunt Nicole wears Uncle Rob's shirts to bed. How they look at each other. How once in a while, he'll drop cash on the counter for us to get a pizza or something so he can take her to dinner. I don't know how old they are or how long they've been married, but he's so good to her.

The other morning they stood in the dining room together in their pajamas. He held her against him, her eyes were closed, and his chin rested on her head. It felt like too private a moment to interrupt, but I stood and watched longer than I should have.

A smile fills my face. I know what to draw. My paper isn't the best, and my pencil isn't quite right for this kind of thing, but I have to get the sketch down.

"Joy." Aunt Nicole's eyes are wide. "I didn't know you even..."

I stare at my bare feet on the carpet. "I drew this just for fun. I..."

"Wow." Uncle Rob looks over his wife's shoulder and then up to me with the same look of disbelief. "I had no idea."

"Do you have drawings? From your mom's house?" Aunt Nicole asks.

"The police took them."

"We should get them back. It seems a—"

"I don't want those. I never want those. I'll draw new ones." I look at Uncle Rob and then Aunt Nicole. "Okay?"

They exchange a glance.

"This is amazing. Thank you so much for sharing this with us." Aunt Nicole's arms come around me in a hug and then Uncle Rob's. I never would have thought that I'd want to be held like this. And now I can't imagine a life when it never happens.

THIRTY-ONE
BACK TO THIS

I don't want to be at school today, where I'm suddenly being looked after by Tara or Justin between classes. Tyler's thrown a few looks my way and so has Trent. I'm still not sure what I did to make them mad, and I don't want to lean on Justin and Tara the way I do, but at least I have people.

I'm silent on the walk home. Justin holds my hand, like usual. I hate that one stupid kid at my school has the power to strip away some of what I've gained in my months here. I can feel anger starting to roll around inside me. Better that than fear. I'm exhausted with fear.

"You want company today?" he asks.

"Maybe later." Right now I need some time alone.

"See you." He pulls us to a stop.

His eyes and his touch send these waves through me. If I let my guard down around him, I'll be in deep fast.

"See you." I give his hand a squeeze and walk toward the front door.

I'm looking forward to the quiet of my room. Trent's car is here, but so is Aunt Nicole's.

I step into the entry. Trent's next to the door with yet a different girl, probably my age, maybe even younger. My jaw clenches at the sight of him.

I make my way to the kitchen as quickly as possible, keeping my eyes on the floor.

I steal a glance behind me as I scan the pantry for a snack.

"So I guess I'll see you later." He kisses her again, in such an obnoxious way, pressing his body against hers, and pinning her against the wall.

"Thanks, Trent. I had fun." She sorts of glances up at him and then down and then she doesn't seem to know where to look.

How can he not see these signs? I need to say something, I just have no idea how to talk to him.

The girl steps out the door and he closes it behind her. I pull a yogurt out of the fridge and a spoon out of the drawer, ready to make a run for my room if I need to. I don't see Aunt Nicole, but he and I both know she's here somewhere so Trent shouldn't be too much of a jerk.

"Hey." He barely glances at me.

"You should be nicer to girls," I blurt before thinking. She's like number four or five this year. I'm clutching my spoon and yogurt so tight my knuckles are white.

He smiles a mischievous grin and jerks open the fridge door. "I thought I was being *really* nice."

The compulsion to speak takes over again because I'm completely annoyed that he doesn't get the kind of pressure he's putting her under. "Not when she only *half* wants to be doing what you want to be doing."

"How would you know that?" He turns toward me and lets out an exasperated sigh. *He's* exasperated with *me?*.

"Because I have a *lot* of practice with guys doing things to girls they *don't want!*" I can't believe my volume. I just yelled at Trent. I'm not afraid of him. My hands are tight. My breathing is shallow and hard.

Now he's staring. His face sort of falls.

I let my shoulders drop when I realize how blatantly I hinted at my past. "Sorry. I shouldn't have yelled."

"Can I ask you something?" His voice is suddenly quiet, like his dad's.

I wait.

"What happened to you? Why is your mom in jail? How did you get out of there?" He's so still. Our eyes are locked.

"That's kind of a long list of questions." Where would I even start?

We stare at each other across the kitchen for a few moments, and suddenly I want to tell him.

"My mom was terrible to me, and she let other people be terrible to me too. The further I am from the situation, the more horrific it seems. Is that what you wanted to know?" My voice still sounds so harsh, *strong*. I feel a surge of pride at how forward I'm being.

His eyebrows come together like he's thinking about this. "Yes… no…How did it stop?"

"Oh." I loosen my grip on my spoon and yogurt. This I can answer. It's the moment everything changed. Terrifying then, but now I realize those moments should have been full of hope instead of fear. "Mom was expecting something in the mail. She gave me her keys to check the box. It was one of the few things she'd let me leave the house for."

"Why?" His whole upper body is tilted toward me now, listening.

"Why what?"

"Why didn't she let you leave the house?"

"I have no idea. I'd make myself crazy if I started asking *why* for everything that happened to me." That would be a horrible, never-ending cycle.

His face is like stone. I don't know if anything about me was real to him before now, just inconvenient because he was suddenly stuck sharing his house and his car and his parents…

"I went out to the mailboxes and the postal worker was still putting envelopes out." I still remember everything. Every word. Every movement. "I'd forgotten about the new burns on my arm." I can see the two small marks, just like they happened yesterday. The smell of dust and hot air and exhaust from her truck. I almost ran back inside when I saw that the mail lady was still there, but Mom had asked me to check the mail, so I didn't want to go back without it.

"Burns?" His question pulls me from the memory.

"Yeah, from cigarette ends." I turn away from him and pull the sleeve of my T-shirt up so he can see the scars there.

His eyes widen. "Those are all from your mom?"

"Almost."

"And your dad?"

"I don't know who he is. If the guys Mom brought home were any indication of who he was, I don't want to know my dad." How am I so calm about all of this? Maybe because I can see how shocked Trent is. Maybe I'm letting *him* take the hurt, instead of me.

His jaw drops. He couldn't just believe before. He had to see and know and hear it all for himself.

"The mail lady looked down at my arm and asked me what happened. I didn't have a ready answer. My bruises and burns were probably one of the reasons Mom never let me leave the house." It's so different telling Trent about this in a place where I feel safe instead of stammering to a stranger and not knowing how to answer. "I told the woman standing there with armloads of mail where the burn came from. She asked if that was normal and I started talking and couldn't stop." Sort of how I'm blurting things out now. "She wouldn't let me go home."

The memory is still sharply painful. I wish I could go back and tell that younger version of myself that I did the right thing.

"The mail lady called the police and I was taken…" He doesn't need every bit of truth. How I was locked up in a strange place while they figured out what to do with me. Questioned. Drugged up so they could examine me after I told them about Richard. "Into child services. Aunt Nicole drove down to California a few days later and picked me up. Mom was arrested and now..."

"Now you're here." His voice is so quiet.

"Now I'm here."

His head tilts to the side as he looks at me, and he licks his lips a few times. "Where would you be if we didn't exist?"

This is the first time I've seen something that looks like sympathy on his face.

"I don't know. I'm barely holding on to the idea that I might get to stay here. Foster home somewhere."

"But they wouldn't have been able to do for you what my parents have done."

"No. I mean, there are some great foster homes out there. But your parents...They're pretty awesome." I can't imagine not being at my aunt and uncle's house.

He stuffs his hands in his pockets. "I'm sorry. I didn't know."

"Yeah, well." I shrug. "It's not like we talk much."

His eyes shift away from mine to look out the window and then at the floor. "I probably haven't been the most understanding."

"It's okay." Without hearing my story from me, I don't think he'd understand.

"You won't have to worry about Tyler anymore. He's just being a prick like he likes to be." Now Trent's eyes are on me.

"It's fine." I shake my head.

"No, Joy." His eyes widen. "It's not fine. Next time he bothers you, just tell him to screw off."

"It's not that easy." I swallow. When my body shakes and I can't breathe, telling someone to screw off doesn't seem possible.

"Then I will." Trent shrugs and steps closer to me. "And since we're cool now, tell Justin to keep his hands off of you."

I laugh at the absurdity of his request. "What?"

"Same rule applies to Tara." He smirks. "No boys. We're not nice."

"Yeah, Trent. I'll remember that." I shake my head. He's so weird. But one conversation made us okay. Kind of cool.

Justin and I sit cross-legged, facing each other on my living room floor. "Trent and I talked." I open and close the small barrette in my hands for something to do.

"How did that go?"

"I think he's finally starting to understand a little." My eyes stay on my hands.

"Understand what?"

"What it was like to grow up as Joy. And why I'm as weird as I am." I let my eyes find his and I smirk.

He shakes his head. "You're not weird."

"You know what's funny?" I start with the barrette again.

"What?"

"His jaw dropped when I showed him the scars, and my Uncle Rob cried over the same thing, but that's such a small part of my old life. It's the part that bothers me the least." I feel hollowed out, but I'm glad that he has another piece of me.

"It's that they can see…" Justin's eyes are curious.

I roll my eyes. "If you wanna see, just ask."

"I…" But for once, Justin doesn't know what to say.

I turn away from him and pull down the neck of my T-shirt so he can see my upper back.

Instead of saying anything, his fingers softly touch the marks on my skin, weaving through the patterns, or connecting the dots. His warm hands send shivers through me.

"So, how is this not the worst part?" he whispers.

I let go of my T-shirt and turn to face him. "Because almost everything else that happened to me was worse." What I've shared so far now feels minor. This feels huge.

His fingers are now touching my cheek, touching my hair. The way his eyes rest on me makes me feel beautiful in that amazing way that starts inside. I have never been touched this way—like he likes me, wants me, but…He's so soft, so gentle, and the designs he traces up my arms and across my back start a thick tingling in my stomach. For the first time since the night he kissed me, I want to try it again.

"Dude!" Trent yells from the entry as he bursts through the door. "Keep your hands off my sister!" He laughs.

Justin pulls away but he's smiling.

"Get out, Trent!" I yell back.

"What's going on out here?" Aunt Nicole steps in.

"What's going on is you're not supervising these two." Trent laughs again as he points at us. He pecks his mom on the cheek and jogs toward the kitchen.

"I trust Justin." She winks at us before turning back toward Trent. "It's you we're all worried about."

"Don't worry about me," he calls over his shoulder. "I'm back with Caitlynn."

Aunt Nicole's eyebrows go up. "Oh."

I don't know why this is a big deal.

Aunt Nicole leans into the living room. "Caitlynn is Mormon and barely lets him touch her, but they've been close for a long time."

Sounds like the perfect girlfriend for worried parents.

"You two have fun...And keep the door open." Aunt Nicole follows after her son.

"You're just like one of the family now, huh?" Justin says.

The thought overwhelms my chest and bursts inside me with happiness.

Maybe I am.

THIRTY-TWO
SHOPPING WITH DAISY—ENOUGH SAID

I'm relieved to know that when I shop with Daisy, holding clothes up and stretching them halfway around our bodies is just as good as trying them on. We're in a huge store that has as many skateboards and rollerblades as clothes. Just walking around is sort of an experience in how art meets skateboarding.

I spot white shoes that look like Justin's and grab a pair.

"Ohh…" Daisy points at the shoes. "Vans. Gonna art them up? Or maybe you should have Justin do it."

"Maybe I will." The idea that he might do that for me…It's personal and close and I'm sure I'm grinning like an idiot.

"He's a nice guy. I'm glad you two are…" She's searching for information; it's all over her face.

"Close." That's safe. I'm learning that I don't have to say everything to give an honest answer.

"That's so cute." She wrinkles up her nose. She's making fun, which is okay. "He's toned down a lot over the last year or so."

"Oh." I know he sort of stopped hanging with the party crowd already, but I'm still not sure what to say.

"Did you know your aunt gave us three hundred dollars?" she asks as we continue to wander through the racks of the crowded shop.

"Wow." It's so much. I didn't pay attention. Daisy just came in like a whirlwind to see if I wanted to shop, and I stood there so stunned at her showing up that Aunt Nicole handed the money to Daisy, not me.

"You totally scored with your aunt and uncle. Except Trent's, like, snottier every week."

"Maybe because he has a different girlfriend every week," I point out.

"Ooh. Joy does have a mean streak in her." Daisy flops a pile of T-shirts, hoodies, and jeans onto the counter.

"I think Trent and I are okay now. He's back with Caitlynn." I look over the mountain of clothes again. "Please say that some of this is yours."

"Yep." She grins. "For my personal shopper fee."

"Daisy!?" A girl in a teeny skirt and tight green hoodie to match the green stripe in her hair pushes into the store.

"Reeeessa!" Daisy takes two leaping steps and throws her arms around her.

But now the excited moment is over, and I feel like I'm watching something personal and have to turn away.

The cashier looks away and shakes her head with a smile.

I catch them again out of the corner of my eye. They're not

kissing but their faces are close, and I don't know what to think.

"Is that normal?" I whisper across the counter to the girl I don't know.

"For Daisy?" Her eyebrows go up. "Everything is normal."

Okay. Good to know. Not that I care, but never knowing what to expect makes me remember how much I don't know about being around people.

"Well, it's easy to see who you went shopping with." Aunt Nicole smiles as I hit the bottom step. "Does that feel better on you?"

I look down. My jeans are a little more torn up—they came that way. I have a T-shirt from a band I'm starting to love, and my hoodie is striped inside with small thumbholes to keep my sleeves down and my hands warm. "I guess I'm also trying to figure out what's better on me."

"Join the club, Joy." She turns into the kitchen. "Every woman I know is trying to figure out what's better on her."

I follow. "When Justin and I talked, he said I was Joy, the girl on a journey of self-discovery." The memory of one of our first small moments fills me up with a warmth I'm still getting used to.

"I really like Justin." She pulls a glass from the cupboard. "As worried about him as I was, I think he's been good for you." She leans onto the counter and rests her chin on her palm.

"Me too." Just thinking about him makes me feel light, floaty. I flip open my phone so I can send him a text. I'd really like him to do my shoes. Maybe I could art up his next pair in trade.

"And Joy?"

"Yeah?" I look over my phone.

"We're *all* on a journey of self-discovery."

"Thanks." So I guess some things are universal.

Justin slides an arm loosely over my shoulders as we walk to the cafeteria.

"Gonna let me sit with you today?" he teases.

"Yep." We slide into seats next to Tara's friends, our table backing the one he normally sits at. Voices echo in the large space like always, but when I look around I wonder how this was ever overwhelming. I remember that feeling, but it's so removed it feels foreign.

I pull out my lunch of carrots and chips. Nicole packed a pudding, but it's probably more for Justin than for me. Not the healthiest lunch, but snacking on finger foods is better than eating nothing. I'm pretty sure in another month I'll think my weirdness over eating messy foods in busy places will also feel like a memory.

Justin reaches over and takes one of my carrot sticks. Tara's friends are huddled over Tara's phone, probably over some Facebook drama, and Justin's friends are cackling behind us.

"This is a really good normal for me," I say.

Justin kisses my shoulder. "Good. You're not going to eat your pudding are you?"

I narrow my eyes. "Maybe just a bite."

"Cool." He tears open the top, dips his finger in the goo, and I laugh a little.

"Hey, Joy." Trent taps my shoulder.

I spin around and see him and Tyler standing together.

I clutch Justin's hand.

But both Trent and Tyler seem relaxed, so I'm definitely curious as to why they stopped.

"So this Friday me and Tyler and a few of the guys thought it would be fun to do a movie night."

"Oh."

"You two wanna join in?" Tyler asks.

Justin's smile is adorable because I can tell he knows exactly what's going on here, and that Trent and Tyler must have had some kind of talk about me or something. It's Trent's way of showing me that Tyler won't bother me anymore.

"We're good," I say.

"But thanks," Justin adds. "Catch ya later."

The guys leave and Justin leans over to me. "What did you do?"

"Told Trent he was being a jerk."

Justin kisses my shoulder again. "That would only work coming from you."

Maybe. But really Trent is just a better guy than I thought he was. That's all.

THIRTY-THREE
THE INJUSTICE OF JUSTICE

The misty rain dampens my hair and face as Justin and I walk home from school together.

"You'll be soaked," he warns.

"I won't care." I smile.

"Hopefully I'll have my car running tomorrow."

"I still won't mind the wet."

He chuckles. "And your shoes. I'm sort of nervous to draw all over them, you know?""

Now it's my turn to laugh. "Don't be."

My driveway comes up way too fast today, but I know he has plans with his dad to work on his car. I step in closer to Justin and breathe in. I wonder if it would be weird to ask him if we could trade shirts. The one of his I have smells like my lavender laundry detergent instead of Justin.

"Tomorrow," he says.

"Tomorrow." I step back and push my damp hair off my face as

I walk through the front door.

The house is so quiet. I wander to the kitchen in search of Aunt Nicole. This place used to feel so big and scary to me, and I can barely imagine that now. I pull open the fridge, and it's filled with food. Aunt Nicole must have gone shopping. I grab a cup of yogurt and take it to the dining room because I like the view of the street.

I stop at the dining room doorway. The air is thick. Aunt Nicole is dabbing her eyes. Uncle Rob has his arm over her shoulders, which wouldn't be strange except he's supposed to be at work.

My heart drops. "Please just tell me whatever is going on now."

Aunt Nicole's voice shakes. "It's fine, Joy. I mean we were kind of expecting this and…"

My body's weak. Shaking. But not out of fear, out of dread for whatever they're going to say. I need to sit and take the chair closest to me.

"Your mom wants a trial. We got the subpoena today. The DA from Bakersfield will be calling you and going over your testimony before we leave," Uncle Rob says.

"Go…*down?*" My legs are weak. Not home. Not there. I can't face her. I'm not ready. I won't ever be ready. Not for this.

"They need you to testify." Uncle Rob sighs.

"But I don't want to. I don't care if nothing happens to her as long as I never have to see her again." The crimes were against *me. I* should be able to decide what happens.

Uncle Rob and Aunt Nicole exchange glances. Aunt Nicole scoots into the chair next to me, resting her hands over mine. "That's not how it works, Joy. The state of California is prosecuting your mother. You're not only the victim, but the witness. Richard, the last man who..."

But his name blocks out the rest of what she says. I'm shaking everywhere. My body won't be able to stay upright in the chair any longer. It requires too much concentration, too much effort. My stomach seizes up. I can't face him again. Ever. Not him, not my mom. I knew this new life was too good to be true. All the horror from my home before is going to be thrown back at me.

"Joy? Did you hear me?" Aunt Nicole asks.

I shake my head. My lips are numb. I can't feel my face.

Her hand wipes my cheek. Am I crying?

"I'll be right back." Uncle Rob stands up and leaves the room.

"I don't have to see her, right? Or him? Or..." My hands clutch my stomach as if that will make it all better.

She lets out a breath. "He pled out, remember? But he'll be a witness at your mom's trial. We've already spoken with the DA. He'll be in custody, so you won't see him. You won't pass him in the hallways. Nothing."

But he'll be there. I'll *feel* him. "My mom?" My voice comes out in a squeak.

"I'm sorry, Joy. We're trying to get you to be able to testify from another room, but it might not work."

"I'll have to be in the *room* with her? In the *courtroom* with her?" I'm angry. Beyond angry. "I've already had to live it once!" I'm yelling but my voice is screechy and hoarse. "And now I have to remember it all again? In front of strangers? In front of *her?*" *In front of you. And then you'll know everything, and how will you feel about me?*

My body breaks down into sobs I can't control. Uncle Rob hands me a small white pill and a glass of water, and kneels on the floor next to me.

How am I supposed to swallow that thing when I can't breathe? I gasp for air a few times. My eyes squeeze tight. All of my senses are being bombarded at once. My ears are loud with the noise of my gasping and the blood thundering through my body. I swear every cell is in protest. Angry. Desperate. Afraid.

"This is ridiculous. I can't believe they're making her do this." Uncle Rob's voice sounds broken, hopeless.

I grab the pill from the table and stuff it in my mouth. Right now I'd take anything for some relief.

"Let's get you to the doctor." Uncle Rob starts to stand.

I shake my head frantically.

"Can I get you to your room?"

I shake my head again. I feel too terrible for that room. As if just by being in there, I'll taint my happy place.

"Why don't we do something absurdly normal?" His hand rests on my shoulder. "Let's watch a movie while we wait for that pill to catch up to you, okay? I can go out to get something to eat, and we'll have a big movie marathon night. Can we do that?"

"Don't go anywhere, okay?" My voice sounds better, less screechy. I'm completely powerless, but I have Uncle Rob and Aunt Nicole. My eyes find his.

"There you are." Uncle Rob attempts a smile, still looking a bit wide-eyed and desperate.

"Here I am." But how long will I stay? I know I'm stronger than I was when I first got here, but I'm not strong enough to do this.

When I wake up in the morning, I'm still on the couch. I'm in my clothes from the night before with my comforter draped over me. Uncle Rob is asleep in the lazy boy. He stayed down here with me. All night.

The weight of what I'm facing still makes breathing hard, no matter how many people I have to stand with me.

The way I feel torn apart is supposed to be getting easier.

None of my lists matter anymore. The things I'm working on. The things I can do. The things I still have a hard time with. Even my list of reasons I'm not crazy seems like a pathetic attempt for me to feel less of the weight that I do. It has nothing to do with my mental state anymore. It has to do with horrible things that happened to me that shouldn't have happened. Things that I'm going to have to testify and talk about in a room full of people. This is all that matters right now. And there's no way out.

THIRTY-FOUR
I DO NOT WANT TO DO THIS

○ I don't know how to face my mother

○ It feels like I'll be crushed into bits if I have to be in the same room as her

○ Richard will be so close

○ My old house

○ My old life

○ All coming back

○ I knew it. I knew I didn't belong here. They will see where I belong, and will they want me back after that?

I wrap my arms around Daisy as soon as I walk in the door to do my last night of kung fu before leaving. And then we end up trying to squeeze each other until I yell give.

"What's up with you?" She chuckles as she pulls away.

"Have to leave next week. My mom's on trial for stuff she did to me, and I have to go and testify." I shrug. That's a great way to show I'm totally okay with going, even though I'm not.

"Sucks." Daisy makes a face. "You know what will make you feel better?"

"Kickin' some ass?" I laugh.

"You got it." She takes my hands in hers and shakes my arms until it shakes my shoulders and my body.

I'm laughing.

"Better?" She giggles.

"I guess." I can't be as heavy as my body wants to be when she's around.

"Perfect." She loops her arm through mine and we head to the front and center. If we're going to be working extra hard today, we might as well be recognized for it.

The DA emailed PDFs of my statements to look over before we go down. It's like reading someone else's life, someone else's story. Only I have pictures and memories and feelings associated with the details laid out on those pages.

It's horror really. Something fit for TV drama, not for a real person's life. I'm still in shock over the things that happened to me. The things I didn't know weren't normal.

And now that I know what normal can be, I'm amazed I survived.

I slide the papers with my statements into the folder Aunt Nicole gave me as the family moves into the dining room.

I'm not sure what's going on, but suddenly we're all sitting at the table.

"My sister, your Aunt Diana, will come in a few days," Uncle

Rob says as he clasps his hands.

Nicole pats my hand, which still rests on the top of the folder, and I give her a smile.

"Why can't we go with you?" Tara asks.

Aunt Nicole lets out a sigh. "Because we don't know how long we'll be gone. Joy's talked with all her teachers and has homework lined up and…"

"But we could do that too," Trent says.

"Sorry, guys." Aunt Nicole shakes her head.

"Mom." Tara's voice gets my attention. It's so serious. "You and Dad are the ones who said we're all going to be a family with Joy. We want to do this with her."

"I agree." Trent leans back in his chair and winks at me.

Uncle Rob and Aunt Nicole exchange glances across the table.

I start to smile, first at Tara, then at Trent.

"This better not be a ploy to skip out of school. And if we need to be in California for more than a week, you two come home. Understand?" Uncle Rob says.

Tara smiles wide. Trent nods in satisfaction. And I sit sort of stunned that they all want to be a part of this.

Running up the hallway of my old house. My legs don't work. Part of me recognizes this might be a dream. I push and pull on my lids, but they won't cooperate. Mom screams my name. Loud. I push harder with my legs, but this hallway is too long when I'm dreaming. I can see the front door now. It's so close. Almost

there, almost there. I'm reaching for it, but Mom's hand grabs my arm sending me flying to the floor.

Failure.

THIRTY-FIVE
KNOW YOU HAVE THAT

Justin and I sit shoulder to shoulder against the wall in the den. I'm wearing the shoes he drew on for me. They're an odd mix of small patterns and abstract shapes, all tiny and detailed. I'm so glad I had him do my shoes instead of me. My leg rests against his and our fingers are laced. If Justin and I are together, our hands are together. This closeness is what I can do. My leg resting against his is new since yesterday, and I love that sitting with him doesn't feel like I'm trying so hard anymore.

"How long will you be gone?"

"I'm not sure. The DA said she'll try to get me in and out of there as fast as she can, but she has no control over the defense and what they want to do or ask or whatever." I suck in a breath. Just thinking about being forced to testify sends a chill through me.

"I wish I knew what to say to make you feel better. You're tougher than you think you are. I know that much."

I lean my head lean on his shoulder. This is new for me. For us.

Like each time we're together, I can do one more thing. Not that he's keeping track. Or if he is, I haven't noticed. But as I soak up his warmth, I can't believe I've never rested my head on him before.

Justin feels like...comfort. His fingers never stop moving—he slides them over my hands, through my fingers, and up my arm. Every touch from him sends tingles through my body—the kind I'm learning to love.

"I'm scared about seeing her, being in the same room as her. I'm afraid to talk about things I haven't had to think about for a long time."

When I tell Justin things I don't tell people, I feel like I'm giving some of myself to him. The easiness I'm starting to feel around him makes talking easier than I would have thought possible. And I can tell he loves it because of how he looks at me or touches me when I admit something—any of the million things that make me feel crazy.

He puts my hands together, almost like he wants me to pray. Palm to palm, fingers outstretched. He rests his hands over mine in the same position.

"This is Joy. Inside here. No one can touch her. She has protection, see?" His hands press into mine, keeping them flat together.

I'm confused. "But you won't be there."

"My hands aren't *me*." He chuckles. "Not really. This just shows how strong you are. You have this shell around you when you need it. That armor made me afraid to talk to you when you first came to school. It made you jump off the dock at Daisy's house, and it makes you one of the tough girls in your martial arts class. The real Joy's still in here, and I love to see her—like right now—but you have all this protection and you don't even know it. So, I guess, just know it. Know you have that."

I stare at our hands together. His covering mine. I have strength. I have protection. I can do this. When our eyes meet again I feel it in my stomach and try to scoot closer, but I'm already there. *Close.*

"I need to get home." He sighs.

"Then I'll walk you out." I stand quickly and wait for him as he stands. It's easier now to keep my eyes on his, and we smile wide before we walk onto the porch together.

My breath comes out in puffs of soft clouds in the cold air.

"I'll miss you." Justin's finger brushes my cheek.

My heart's thundering in my ribs. "Me too."

I lean toward him and his lips touch my forehead. Now both his hands are in my hair, and every touch, every movement from him sends familiar tingles across my skin, but now they're shooting around like electricity. His breathing and my breathing is the only thing I hear. My hands rest on either side of his neck, our faces are still touching. No way my heart can continue to stay in my chest the way it's beating right now. I've never wanted to be with someone the way I want to be with him.

His nose touches my cheek. "I'm falling for you, Joy."

There's no stopping my smile. "I know how it feels," I whisper. I tilt my face just slightly, just until our lips brush together. No more tingles, a wave of something completely new washes through me.

I love the rush, but it scares me all at the same time. The wave of feeling urges me to be closer, pressed against him. But I can't. Not yet. "See you soon."

"Soon."

Despite the protests from my body, I step back. Justin's eyes hit mine one last time before he walks out of the light of the porch and into the darkness. I hope I'm not gone long.

THIRTY-SIX
TRANSFER

We take Uncle Rob's SUV because it has three rows of seats. Whoever's in the way back seat gets to lie down. Right now it's me.

Uncle Rob got me three sketchbooks and so many art pencils that I'm not sure what to do with them all. I thought all the new stuff would make me feel pressured to draw, but it doesn't. It makes me crave it. I've sketched Daisy in kung fu, the shadows of the people around the fire the night I jumped into the lake, anything that pops into my head.

I've drawn my hand mixed with Justin's hand. I've drawn Lydia with her smirk, the one she uses when she's trying to make me feel better about not taking my crap. I've drawn Tara a bunch of times. I love her cheeks and smooth figure. Trent's been harder, but I've drawn him a few times too. One with him and Caitlynn that he posted on his wall. Caitlynn thinks it's super sweet. He's so different around her. I don't know what changed for Trent earlier this year, and I don't know what changed for him later, but I feel better being around him now. He's more like his dad.

I started drawing house plans, just to try it out. Uncle Rob gave me a list of all the standard stuff like hallway and doorway widths, closet depths, and specs for bathroom spaces. I've drawn three small homes and I love each of them.

These pictures are all my new life. The life I can't imagine not having anymore. The life I want to keep forever. I need to focus on this part of my life to keep me from thinking about all the things that are completely out of my control.

"So our hotel rooms connect." Aunt Nicole pulls open the door between the two rooms. "We can work this however we want. Kids in one room, us in the other room. We can all sleep in the same space. If Joy needs time"—her eyes wander to mine—"you can have a room, but you can't be alone. Not now. Not for something like this."

"I'm not that fragile." But maybe I am. The thought that they don't want to take the risk of me being alone makes me feel good, loved. Not embarrassed like the attention used to. I'm not even sure when that happened or what changed, but feeling this loved is something I couldn't have imagined before now.

"Doesn't matter." Nicole smiles. "Let's get something to eat. We have a long day tomorrow."

A long day. I can't even think about tomorrow.

Uncle Rob steps back toward the door. "Joy and I are going out to get food. We'll be back."

I follow Uncle Rob out of the hotel room. It's not hot this time of year, but the dust and dryness still hit my nose the way they always did.

"Going out okay?" he asks.

I just nod. Being back here is surreal. Like the new me doesn't belong in this dry place anymore.

We climb into the car and even after the long drive down, I don't mind much. A thought hits me. I know this is going to be a hard week but…"I want to drive by my house."

"What?"

"I—I want to drive by my house." My heart's pounding hard at the thought of seeing it again—the place that seems to be in my dreams more often than not.

"Are you sure that's a good idea?" he asks.

"Nope." I pull my legs to my chest.

He starts the car.

"But I want to do it anyway."

I tell him where to turn. Bakersfield is small so even though I didn't get out much, I know how to get there.

The sign for the trailer park is ahead. I can't go in. But I made it this far. "Stop here."

"Here?" His eyes scan around us. We're on a dirty street, nothing but brown hills in the background and a trailer park that looks half-abandoned.

"That was mine, there." I point to a small white and blue trailer near the back.

"That's where you lived?" Uncle Rob's never been here. Never seen this place.

"That's the only place I remember living until your house."

He rests his elbow on the door and brings his hand to his chin. We sit in silence.

Sitting in front of the house is not as bad as I thought it would be. It's familiar, but feels a lifetime away. The small home doesn't feel as close as it did even two months ago. Back when I was still barely talking.

I don't even mean to, but I get out of the car and start walking. Uncle Rob's next to me in a minute. Will this be good? Or torture? I don't care.

The mailboxes haven't moved, and one of my best memories of this place floods my mind. We walk up the row of houses, all looking much the same. Did these people know? Did anyone know? I'm not sure, and I guess it doesn't make a difference now.

Uncle Rob's arm goes around me. The smell, the dust. I stop two trailers away. Am I a coward for not going any closer? The same small graying wooden porch slants away from the door. The curtains are different. Someone else is in there now. The door opens and I stare.

A little blond girl bounds out with a pink backpack.

"Watch that bottom step, honey! Until we can fix it!" Her mom steps out behind her and locks the door.

She picks up her little girl and gives her a squeeze before putting her in their car. The girl looks so happy. Her mom looks so...nice.

My chest pounds. Another mom and daughter live there and

they look…okay. It wasn't *me*—the things that happened in that house—it was Mom. All of those horrible experiences somehow come back to Mom.

The realization hits me again. Hard. I didn't cause my situations. Mom did. My experiences had nothing to do with this place or our circumstances. Just her. I'll never know why she hurt me, or why she let things happen. Just like I told Trent the other day, the whys would start a spiral I couldn't stop.

The woman buckles her daughter in and waves as she drives past us. I wave back and lean farther into my uncle.

"My life here wasn't fair to me." I actually feel the words and believe the truth of them. I never realized that part of me felt like I deserved what happened. My history seemed too horrible to deserve, but now that I'm letting my past go, I feel relief. I really, actually, deserved better.

"No. None of that life was fair to you." He squeezes my shoulder and kisses the top of my head.

I turn toward the car.

He pulls in a long, deep breath. "Food?"

"Food."

I glance over my shoulder again and keep walking. That's not where I belong. Never was. Never will be again.

The Xanax keeps me from having dreams, but it doesn't help me sleep. Not tonight.

Tara, Trent, and I are all in one room, but the door between our rooms stays open. Uncle Rob comes in several times throughout the night. Checking on me. Making sure I don't slip away.

I'm still here. Still breathing. And still dreading tomorrow.

Uncle Rob, Aunt Nicole, and I have a ridiculous conversation on who will and won't be in the courtroom. Am I comfortable with them there? Do I want them there? Uncle Rob finally tells me to pretend I'm in a world where I'm a completely selfish girl. Now what do I want?

I still want whatever makes them most comfortable.

We come up with a compromise.

They'll sit in the courtroom unless I look at them and shake my head. Then they'll leave. I'm allowed to ask the bailiff to bring them back in. This way, if I have to talk about things I don't want them to hear, they won't. Aside from that, they'll be there.

Tara and Trent will stay at the hotel. I'm relieved. They don't need to know the horrid details of my past. The fact that they're staying in an old Super 8 in Bakersfield is enough.

I wring my hands as I'm led to the stand—nerves twisting inside me as I stare at the floor. I have to be careful about where I look because I'm not sure how I'll react to seeing Mom. I'm separated from the people in the room by a step up and a small wall that's chest height when I sit. I try to make myself feel that separation. My barrier. My safety.

Tension has such a hold on me that my legs ache and I'm trying to remember to breathe. In. Out. In. Out.

There's some talking that I don't catch because I'm counting breaths. I watch the judge with her tight bun and the bailiff and the attorney. Mom's in here. I tighten my hands around each other to stop them from shaking. My heart stops every time I catch her in my peripheral vision.

I mumble my way through promising to tell the truth and trying to focus on the prosecutor. She's short and thin with a friendly face and dark blond hair. She's in a plain navy suit, which almost blends into the background.

Her first questions for me are easy. My name, my birthday. Where I go to school, where I live, how long I've lived there. I'm speaking, which feels like a victory after how hard I concentrated on breathing just a few moments ago.

She asks if I remember the day Mom and I were separated. Only Trent knows this story. I talk about being excited to hold the keys in my hand and getting the mail. I talk about the mail carrier and the look of shock on her face. It feels so much different talking about that situation now. I remember the terror of the day it happened. When I told Trent that memory felt different, more detached. Today the story feels like the huge moment it was. The moment my old life started to break away and my new one began to form.

This story leads into questions about my time with child services and then into specifics on my mother and the people she let into our home. My eyes catch Uncle Rob's and then Aunt Nicole's. They both give me a reassuring smile. Aunt Nicole's eyes are red. I'm not sure about Uncle Rob's. I don't look at them long enough to think about what they might be feeling. There's only room in my heart for my own emotions right now.

If I feel exposed by what I have to share when talking about Mom; I can't imagine how much worse Richard's trial would have been.

I cry three times. Once when I mention the movie *Matilda* and once when I talk about how Mom laughed when I told her I'd been raped. I cry again when we talk about Richard. Mom beat me up. She thought I was trying to steal him away. She didn't believe that I didn't want him in my room. He was in there so much.

Uncle Rob and Aunt Nicole are wiping tears. I forgot to send them out so they didn't have to hear. Or maybe I'm just selfish and want them here.

I stand up and show the jury the scarring on my back. They try not to gasp, but do anyway. So ridiculous. Those marks are the result of a minor discomfort that lasted only a week or two. Funny how people only believe in things they can see, even when I shared so much more. I wish I could tell them about how much more scarred my heart is. How my thoughts sometimes don't feel like my own because I can't control them. How broken I am. My body is just a body, but the rest of me…That's where the damage is.

"I'm finished, Your Honor," the DA says.

"We'll break for lunch for one hour." The judge taps her gavel.

I sit, afraid to move, and stare at my lap. My mom's moving out of the courtroom with the bailiff. Her form barely appears in the outer edges of my vision. I can't look. Not directly.

"Joy?" The attorney steps up to the wooden box, which is starting to feel like a prison. "You were amazing."

"Thanks," I mumble. The jury's gone. Uncle Rob and Aunt Nicole are standing behind the DA's table, waiting.

"After lunch isn't going to be fun. The defense attorney is going to hammer you with anything he feels is a discrepancy. Don't feel bad if you need to ask for a break. Don't feel bad about crying. Just continue to be honest, okay?"

I nod. My body is thick, heavy, tired. How can sitting and talking make me so *tired*?

Uncle Rob's arm is around me as soon as I step down. I follow my aunt and uncle down the white brick hallway into a room where we have a small lunch. I can't eat. After pleadings from Aunt Nicole, I take a few bites of croissant.

"I can't believe…" Uncle Rob starts.

Aunt Nicole silences him with a glare.

"That was just some of what happened." I let my eyes find his. "The DA's only asking me about my mom. I don't have to relive everything."

Uncle Rob's face has fallen further. I'm worried that what I told him made him feel worse instead of better. I thought it was good that I didn't have to talk about everything I remember.

Uncle Rob hands me my phone. "It's been buzzing in my pocket."

Three messages are from Justin.

How are you?

Thinking about you.

Wish I could be there.

I type: *Survived my morning. It sucked. Going to get worse. I'm okay. Promise. Can't wait to see you again.*

Then I hit Send and smile. I can't believe how lucky I am to have so many amazing people in my life.

"Can you tell me where your mother is? Point her out in the room?" I hate the attorney already. He's roundish and balding, and wears a smug look on his doughy face.

My eyes float to Aunt Nicole first. She feels like more of a mom than my mom ever has. "There." I point to my mother, sitting at the defendant's table. But I can't make myself look at her. Not now. Hopefully not ever.

"Who do you live with?"

"My Aunt Nicole and Uncle Rob, but they feel like…"

He holds his hand up. "You've answered, thank you."

My heart sort of breaks. They're like my family. Not her. My eyes go from them to the squidgy attorney in front of me.

His questions are direct and brutal. He insinuates that I tried to make my mom angry. That I did everything in my power to hurt a woman who was already in a fragile mental state.

I'm determined not to cry. I set my jaw and stare at this man who I hate more with every question. I don't realize until the judge calls an end to our day that maybe if I had let myself cry, the attorney might have stopped being such a jerk.

I'm silent when the day is done. Aunt Nicole's silent. Uncle Rob's silent. No one knows what to say. I don't know what to think about the quiet. Tomorrow morning is when the DA gets to ask me questions about anything the defense attorney said or got me to say. At least I don't hate her. But I do hate that I'll have to sit in the same room with my mom again.

Tara and Trent don't ask any questions. They've ordered pizza and two cartoons from the hotel.

I nibble on a slice because I know everyone will worry if I don't, but it takes me nearly an hour to eat it.

"I think I need a..." But I'm suddenly not sure how to ask for one of my panic pills. I'm still not sure how I feel about them, but taking one isn't embarrassing like it once was. It feels okay. Like I'll be able to sleep and not have nightmares. They help me function. Maybe I won't need them forever, but I need them right now.

"You know you can take half?" Uncle Rob hands me one.

"I'll take the other half." Trent winks at me.

I shrug, bite half off, and hand the rest to him. He downs it before either of his parents have a chance to stop him.

"What?" He shrugs at their stares. "I'm curious."

Aunt Nicole is sitting on the bed, her back against the wall. I sit next to her and rest my head on her shoulder. There's singing in the movie. Everyone's dancing and looks happy. It feels so foreign.

"Okay, Joy? Why don't you like these pills again?" Trent asks. "I feel awesome. Already." He laughs a bit, his eyes already half closed.

"It's different when you feel like you need one." I find a smile for him.

"I'm just so…relaxed…and happy…and tired…" He's lying on his bed, stretched out like a starfish.

"You're weird," I say. But it really feels good that Trent gets one more small part of me.

When Aunt Nicole stands, she kicks Trent in the foot. "Don't get used to it."

Uncle Rob takes her place next to me. "You're amazing, Joy," he whispers. "Don't forget that. Ever."

Right. The movie fades and the room fades and my day fades.

I fall asleep with my head on his warm shoulder.

I'm back on the stand in the courtroom. All I want is to go home.

"Tell me about where you live now, Joy." The DA's suit today is a dark green. Still simple and boring.

"I'm with Aunt Nicole and Uncle Rob." This is a good way to start my day.

"Do you feel safe there?"

Immediately tears come down my face. "Yes."

"Why does that make you cry?"

"Because I've never felt safe at home before." I shiver. Why is this simple question such a hard one to talk about?

"Never?"

"No." I wipe my face with the back of my sleeve a few times.

"Why not?"

The defense attorney objects, but she's allowed to ask me the question again anyway.

"Because…" I think of Uncle Rob and Aunt Nicole. I think about how they turned their lives upside down for me and then said how happy they were that I was in their home. And then about Mom and how I had to sneak out of bed to do the dishes so she wouldn't hurt me. "She wasn't a mom to me. She never protected me. Ever." For the first time since taking the stand I let my gaze wander to her. She's looking at me, but not like I'm her daughter, more like I'm a curiosity. She looks older, more tired than I remember. If she ever had any love for me, surely that love would be showing now. "You should have kept me safe. And you didn't. You never did." I'm crying again, but I don't care. I don't bother to wipe the tears or anything. Just let them fall. And I let myself continue to stare.

The defense attorney makes another objection and I watch Uncle Rob and Aunt Nicole whisper to each other while the two attorneys approach the judge.

Without my aunt and uncle, I couldn't do this. I wouldn't be able to talk about my old life without sobbing, if at all. And now I'm facing my mother and wishing I could somehow get the answer to the only question I have for her. *Why?* Only I know that's something I'll never have an answer for.

I stare at Mom, again wondering if she even understands what my life was like compared to what it should have been like.

Mom's eyes float away from mine, but nothing passes across her face. No regret, no sadness. Nothing. Does she really not care?

My body's shaking again, but I'm breathing. And I'm not staring at my feet.

I don't know when I'll be okay with her lack of feeling toward me or if I ever will. Just like the why questions I can't answer, Mom's thought process is something I will never understand.

"Okay," the prosecutor starts. "I was asking about where you live now. Who you're with. You can go ahead."

I gaze at Uncle Rob and Aunt Nicole. Aunt Nicole's wiping tears again, and Uncle Rob has his arm tightly around her. "My aunt and uncle are more like parents than…" *than anything I could think of before I moved in with them.*

"There were some questions asked yesterday about where you lived, and I think your answer was cut off."

I remember the attorney asking about who I lived with, his smug look and shiny head. "I said I lived with my aunt and uncle, and I wanted to say that they feel like my parents. They take care of me. They protect me without a second thought. It's not something I ever expected." I stare down at the shoes Justin drew on for me, knowing this is almost over.

After a few breaths, I'm ready to look up again.

"Thank you, Joy. I think we're done with you." The DA smiles.

I wipe the tears from my face my body weak with relief. I'm done.

The judge speaks. "Joy Neilsons is excused. We're going to break before our next witness, Richard Houston."

My body's cold. Shivery. I need to get out. Now.

The bailiff escorts me down. I search for Aunt Nicole and Uncle Rob. I don't care if Mom's looking at me or not looking at me. My part is done. Over. For real. I'm numb and staring at my feet as I move my legs forward. One at a time.

"I'm so proud of you." Aunt Nicole takes me in a big hug.

My eyes search for Uncle Rob. Richard is in the building somewhere. I need my uncle. I need to feel safe.

"I need to get out of here." My voice shakes.

Uncle Rob's arm comes around me as he leads us out of the building and to the car.

I'm safe. It's done. It's over.

THIRTY-SEVEN
TIME FOR THINKING

There's too much time for thinking on the drive home. Tara's getting texts from a boy at school—she shows me one once in a while. She keeps blushing and giggling as she types into her phone. It's earned more than one odd look from Uncle Rob in the driver's seat. I'm thrilled for her.

Trent's on his phone too. I'm not sure what turned him around, but he seems so much…softer now. Calmer. More mature. I don't know. But he's easier to be around for all of us.

We don't expect the jury to have a verdict for at least a few more days. The outcome doesn't matter to me because I know Uncle Rob and Aunt Nicole will fight to keep me with them, and I won't have to leave. That's all I care about really—keeping my new life.

I lie in the backseat and stare at the ceiling. Despite feeling like Mom is just in my past, I'm not sure if I know how to keep my past behind me. Maybe my experiences should be back there, stuffed away—maybe not. I don't want to hurt anymore. I don't want the feeling of loss over my mother or the feeling of not being able to control what she did or didn't do for me, but getting rid of that feeling is going to take time. I sat in the courtroom and I don't know how to describe my feelings toward her. I wanted to get away, to get out. To not have to face her. But in some ways, I face her every day. I face her because she's part of each of my fears. I know my fears won't disappear overnight, but I'm ready to start letting some of them go.

In time, right? Isn't that what everyone says? It'll all heal in time. I guess what I'm ready to say is that my experiences with my mother no longer define my life, who I am. *I* define that now.

I'm the daughter of Uncle Rob and Aunt Nicole. We talked about me calling them Mom and Dad, but I find myself avoiding situations where I have to use their new names. That will come. Hopefully soon.

There are other things that are starting to define who I am. I'm the girl who draws, who does kung fu. The quiet girl. The girl who jumped in the lake with Daisy. The girl who hopes for a life filled with adventures of her choosing and even some adventures that feel unexpected. Because, for as many things as I feel like I don't have control over, there are just as many that I do.

I'm still Joy, the girl on a journey of self-discovery, and I hope to always be that girl.

THIRTY-EIGHT
A HAPPY BEGINNING

We pull into our driveway. In our car. In front of *our* house. It's nearly midnight, but Justin said he's up. Uncle Rob seems concerned about me walking over there so late. Aunt Nicole said it's simply that he doesn't like the idea of either of his daughters around any boys. Ever.

The streetlamps light the way, and they all seem to have halos from the misty rain. My legs aren't working right after the long drive, but I feel like a whole new person. Testifying is as close to my old life as I'll ever have to get. Ever again. I did it. I can do anything.

"Hey you," Justin says, and I jerk my head up to see him on the sidewalk in front of me. Smiling.

"I said I was coming." I don't even try to slow my grin. My hair is still pulled up and it feels good to be exposed like this.

"I wouldn't be much of a nice guy if I made you walk all that way." He smirks and then his face softens. "I missed you."

"A lot?"

"A way lot. Like…I don't know. Like I've never missed anyone."

His fingers slide through mine as soon as I'm close enough. He stays his normal distance, keeping space between us. I don't need that space anymore—or at least not as much. I think this is one of the first fears I want to try to put behind me.

I pull him closer. Our stomachs touch. My chest presses against his. All those electric tingles are back, the ones like from our last night on the porch together.

Our breathing is all I can hear. He tilts his head to be even closer.

I close my eyes. I'm strong. I choose this. "I really, really want a kiss from you."

His cheek rests against mine, and I want this from him. I want his arms around me. I want him to be close to me. Justin's lips press against mine, so softly—too softly. I part mine and kiss him again and then again. And now my arms are pulling on him more tightly, and I can't imagine why I'd ever want to let him go.

"I'm dizzy." He chuckles, breathless. His lips touch my cheek as he talks.

"I'm okay now. Really, actually okay," I say. He feels good. I'm still holding him as close as my arms will allow. "Or heading there anyway."

"So I can hold you the way I want to?" he asks.

"Mm-hmm…" But I'm dizzy too.

His arms tighten around me and I love the feeling. It's not suffocating—it's warm and it's what I *want*. I tilt my face toward him and his lips meet mine again.

And right now, I totally deserve this. To be this happy. He's falling and I'm falling too, and I'm determined to love every minute of it. Because, even though I really want him to catch me at the bottom, if he doesn't, I have people who will.

THIRTY-NINE
THE SORT OF END

The hall is the same dingy white as I remember. There are dark, tense voices. Someone's coming my way. I don't care. I'm not in a hurry. My legs feel okay. Strong. I take about ten steps to the door, pull it open, and step outside into the sun. Just like that.

"Yahtzee again?" Trent frowns and raises an eyebrow at me.

"Yeah." I smirk. "I got home on time, so I get to choose."

He chuckles. "Fine, fine…"

Caitlynn laughs next to him. She has a kind face, bright eyes. I liked her immediately.

"Apparently you always win anyway, right?" I raise a brow at him.

"I used to."

Until me. I know this is true.

"So are we ready?" Dad asks.

"Yep."

"Hurry, up. I got curfew." Justin kisses my cheek.

I blush at his very public display of affection.

"Dad, aren't you going to call her on that?" Tara winks as my eyes catch hers.

"Call me on what?" I check each of the faces around the table.

"No PDA allowed in the house," she explains.

"Is it really public if we're in the house?" I look toward Mom and Dad as I pass out the scorecards.

"Yes." They answer at the same time. But both are smiling and look at me with more love than I ever expected.

Justin looks down embarrassed. Tara and Trent laugh.

Justin's hand reaches for my leg under the table, squeezing my knee to show he doesn't mind the teasing and that he's happy to be here. This is my normal.

And it's true what I read about joy. It's the kind of happiness that not only fills you up but spills over. Really, all you have to do is look for it, and then have the strength to let it in. And believe it or not, that's the hardest part.

ACKNOWLEDGMENTS

I woke up one Saturday morning with the first line of this book stuck in my head and had nearly a third of the book written over that weekend. Joy's story wouldn't let me go.

Joy's backstory came about because of a case that my husband brought home from his work as a prosecutor. That case ended in the death of the child, rather than the happy ending like Joy's. There's a bench in my children's school with a plaque that holds this child's name, and my heart breaks a little every time I see it.

Huge thanks to my husband, Mike, who is always a big champion of my writing. He fell in love with this story and said, "Yes. This is it. This has to get out into the world."

Always a thank-you to Heather Hubb—the girl who works for shoes.

A special thank-you to authors Kaylee Baldwin and Rachael Anderson, who were among my first readers for this story; and to my agent of awesomeness, Jane Dystel, who wrote me back the day after

I emailed her with the MS saying—Let's move forward with this.

Big hugs to author Christa Desir, who kept telling me to hold on to this book until the timing was right—I can't thank you enough. I held on to this manuscript a lot longer than I ever thought I'd be able to.

When a character is this close to your heart, the idea of editing can be terrifying, but Wendy McClure's guidance on this was amazing, as was Kristin Zelazko's, and made me know, once again, that my Joy found her perfect home.

A massive thank you to all the lovelies at Albert Whitman from the editors to the designers to the publicity peoples...Seriously. Thank you.

And lastly, thank you to my parents who are still among the most amazing people I've been privileged to know. You may have not known a *thing* when I was in high school, but you now seem smarter every year. So. Weird.